Judy Jones and the Monkey Man

A Novel
By

J. Michael O'Reilly

Contents

Chapter One - Papa in a Trance

I want to tell you about my father. I know a lot of people will think they know all about him already, having read so much in the papers, and seen it all on TV and on the internet, about how he completely lost his mind and went into a deep and irreversible trance only to become a musical and financial genius who gave piano recitals all over the world and made millions trading the foreign exchange markets. (Yes, I know when I say it like that it sounds like a bit implausible to say the least, but that's how it happened). And you will have heard him referred to by many different names - most commonly Monkey Man; but also Idiot Savant (hated that one); Trader Chimp; the Chopinzee, and the rest. He didn't mind - he had no idea what they were calling him, or indeed what was going on around him, having lost all consciousness of his own self from the time they found him in a catatonic trance on the floor of our holiday apartment in Austria. That was two years ago, a lot has happened since and I'm going to tell you everything. I don't know how it's going to turn out as I have never written anything in my life apart from school stuff, but when the newspapers came after me for my story an agent appeared from nowhere and took over, and now he wants me to write this book so I'd better get on with it.

Bill (that's my agent) seems scary but he's actually really nice and a great agent if of course you need such a thing in your life; it's like having a vicious dog that everyone else is afraid of but he's gentle with me and protects me from the mob, as he seems to call everybody apart from the three of us - Mum, Dad and me that is. Bill's big and hairy with enormous teeth - not sticky out teeth just really big and lots of them, more than you'd need normally. Before he turned up there were all these newspaper articles that called themselves "Exclusive Interview with Judy Jones, Monkey Man's Daughter" (oh that's me by the way, daughter of Jack and Jenny Jones - I know, I know, looks like someone's got themselves a bit of a complex with the letter J) these articles seem to have written themselves, it would appear, as I had nothing to do with them. But I was so mad about some of the things they said that when Bill brought in the book publishers I said I wouldn't let them publish a word about Papa unless I wrote it myself. After a lot of throwing their arms up in horror at such a thought, they finally agreed to let me write the book on my own first and if it was no good this guy they called "the ghost" would sort it out.

I kind of liked the idea of having a ghost so I said OK and they explained how it works. I write the book any way I want and this ghost guy puts it into decent English so it makes sense and people will be able to read it without saying I'm an idiot just like my Dad (sorry Papa, I don't think you're an idiot, but that's what they would say). How difficult could it be to write a book anyway? It's just like talking except you write it down, and anyone can talk. They only gave me one piece of advice regarding the writing and that was to avoid clichés. I thanked them for that and said I would avoid them like the plague. Actually they were quite polite about my literary skills, saying they were sure the book wouldn't need too much re-writing and if it did what could anyone expect from a sixteen-year-old schoolgirl? Yeah, really polite.

One thing I want to say before I start is about the title. The publishers asked me had I got a title and I said no but I would think about it and come up with one before I was finished writing. Then of course they couldn't resist sticking in their tuppence worth - it's remarkable how these people all do the same trick, they ask you first for your opinion on something, "So Miss Jones, have you thought about this?" or "Well Miss Jones, what do you feel about that?" and when you say you don't know because it's the first time you've ever heard of such a thing and need to think about it, then they come out with the answer that they want, expecting you to just agree. They all do this thing - even Bill. Last week one of the girls in his office (right snooty cow this one Annabelle is, can't stand her) rang me up with, "What would you feel about a fifty-date book-signing roadshow?" I mean, what can you reply to that? If you say what they want you to say, which is, "Great, when do I start?" you've no idea what you're letting yourself in for, you could be touring the country for months, signing piles of books till your arm falls off. But on the other hand, if you say you'll have to think about it she treats you like an ungrateful wretch. So when I say I'll get back to her this is what she comes out with: "Oh Bill would expect you to agree to that. It's standard practice in such a campaign." I said I didn't realise I was waging war and I'd have to review my campaign strategy and get back to her.

Anyway the title: so we're all in this meeting in the Publisher's office in the wood-paneled boardroom of a four-story over basement Georgian pile overlooking Bloomsbury Square - though you couldn't really call it an office, it's more like some really old-fashioned dining room in a big old mansion and we're all sitting around this huge, long, mahogany dining table like something you'd see in an old movie but there's nothing to eat - not a sausage - just bottles of expensive French sparkling water and plenty of things to write with. The "Editor" is there, and the "Editorial Director" and they're both wearing suits, one stripy grey and one plain grey, they've just been introduced to me a minute ago so I've no idea what they're like but stripy looks friendly and plain doesn't; only problem is I've forgotten which one is which, I mean I know which one is stripy and which one is plain, I just can't remember who's the boss - and a couple of pretty girls who haven't been introduced at all so I've absolutely no clue who they are, they could be the suits' girlfriends for all I know. We're discussing the book and after a while we get to the title. So, as I said, they ask me had I got one and as soon as they get the answer they were looking for we're off to the races. First the polite deference to my wishes in the matter and then one of the pretty girls takes a very deep breath and delivers her opinion that, "Considering pre-existing publicity and reader expectations, not to mention commercial viability and the visibility factor as outlined in our exclusively-commissioned publicity department's public relations poll, we find that the most appropriate buyer-friendly and sales-enhancing title would be:

'Monkey Man' ". At that point of the meeting I think I may have had to review my campaign in the Ladies and forgotten to return to the wood-paneled board room of the four-story over basement Georgian pile overlooking Bloomsbury Square until Bill came looking for me.

"Bill, I can't do that to him," I moaned, and I'm embarrassed to admit it but I think I might have blubbed a bit. "He's my father and I'm not doing that to him. Whatever the press have called him, I can't help that, but I am not calling him that myself, not in the title of my book." Bill was very nice as always, and let me go home on my own while he went back to the suits around the mahogany table and told them we'd think about it. I got on the tube in Russell Square and mingling with the crowd I began to feel a bit more normal again. Crowds are great for making you feel invisible. Like Harry Potter I love riding around on trains; I could do it all day and sometimes that's exactly what I do. (For that I find the Circle Line is best - don't know why exactly, it just is.) But believe me, whatever I call the book - and I have a few ideas myself as it happens - it's not going to be anything with a monkey in it.

****

I suppose I better start at the very beginning - a very good place to start as Sister Maria pointed out - and that's quite appropriate because at the beginning of that movie (which Papa and myself must have watched about twenty times when I was between the ages of two and fourteen) as the camera goes over the mountains, in a helicopter I suppose, and the orchestra is warming up with a big long intro, and before you zoom in on Julie Andrews twirling around and belting out, "The hills are alive …" one of the lakes that you see is our lake in Austria. It's called the Wolfgangsee and it was where we had our holiday home and we used to swim in that very lake every summer. Mozart's mother was born in our town on the lake which is called St Gilgen, and they moved to Salzburg when she was a young girl. There she met the handsome young composer and orchestra conductor called Leopold Mozart and the rest as they say is history. So when her first little boy was born it was natural to call him Wolfgang, not after the lake which would be silly, but after the most famous local saint. You see another town on the lake is called St Wolfgang where this holy man founded his first church, and it's been a place of pilgrimage for a thousand years. It would be like calling an English boy George or an Irish boy Patrick. So that is the end of the history lesson and thank you all for listening.

It was also as I have said where my father was found on the living room floor of our beautifully furnished (that was Mum) apartment on the point of death as he hadn't eaten or drunk anything in nearly a week. He had been there on his own for a month after Mum and I had had our holiday with him in July and gone home, her back to work and me to rehearse for some play I had to do. But Dad had a job there, playing the piano in a nice hotel two nights a week, Mondays and Wednesdays (Note to ghost: the days are important otherwise I wouldn't mention them so don't cut them out) so he stayed on. It wasn't much in the way of work but they paid him well, and augmented by a few private English lessons, he could earn more there than he could at home during his long teacher's summer holidays. He must have had his fit and collapsed on the Tuesday or Wednesday but when he didn't turn up to play the piano in his hotel on the Wednesday night they let it pass and did nothing about it; they didn't have a phone number for him I suppose. But when he again failed to show up on the following Monday they finally sent someone to look for him at the apartment building. This delay was to say the least disastrous as it meant that he had been lying on the floor in his trance for almost a week by the time help came. There are some things in life it is hard to forgive, even if they are not really anybody's fault.

The neighbours in the apartment straight across from us said, "Yes, now that we think about it, we haven't seen him for a few days either, yes I suppose it might be a week." So the geniuses start knocking on the door and as they're standing there they start hearing some strange noises emanating (I think is the right word here) from within. When asked later by the paramedics how they knew he was alive and they were asked to describe the noises they heard, they were in complete agreement that they sounded like the chattering of an ape or monkey. This brilliant and original piece of diagnosis was repeated to the examining doctors who picked it up and ran with it for the whole nine yards and then repeated it back to my mother and me until it was firmly entrenched as the most concrete and definite aspect of the unusual symptoms he presented. Unbelievable! Anyway at least from the ape-like chattering they knew he was alive so they got the caretaker to open up and there he was, in a frightful state obviously, I don't want to think about it, it is after all my father we are talking about, and nearly dead from dehydration and heatstroke. The Austrian alpine summer weather is, to be kind, unreliable, and as we knew from our summer holidays there, if you were unlucky you could have nothing but constant rain for two weeks. But it had perversely taken it into its head for this week to be one of the hottest all year, and with the combination of heat, lack of sustenance, and whatever brainstorm he had suffered, the poor man, although only fifty-three and reasonably fit, was nearly done for.

He was immediately rushed to the local hospital where I must say he was treated with great kindness, partly helped by the fact that no less than two of our neighbours in the apartment building actually worked there. Meanwhile my mother and I were informed of the situation at home in Barnes, and of course we were devastated. We were just finishing our dinner, I remember, about half seven it must have been. It was funny with just the two of us but Mum still insisted on us eating in the dining room, "No need to let the standards slip just because your father isn't here," she used to enjoy saying. I was just clearing the table and Mum was opening the paper when the phone rang. I mean the house phone, the landline, which was unusual enough in itself these days as we all had our own mobiles of course. So I went out to the hall to answer it, expecting to have to fob off some poor call centre chap trying to earn his crust by making crank calls on people at dinner time. But it wasn't someone with a list of interesting questions about supermarket advertising he was just dying to ask, it was something far weirder. At first I couldn't make it out at all as the line was a bit wonky and the geezer at the other end didn't appear to be speaking English. Then I worked out that he was looking for Mrs Jones, but what was throwing me was the pronunciation - he kept calling the name Yones. Anyway I said that was me though obviously he wanted Mum, but she's always telling me to take the call and take a message so it was easier than going in to her and being sent back to the phone again. Then things got a bit scary because the next bit I could make out was "plees not to vurry" but my husband had had an accident and he was in hospital.

"Mum!" I screamed, "Quick!" But I didn't want to go get her as the hospital guy was still talking in his funny accent and telling me "plees not to vurry" but I should fly to Austria as quickly as possible and come to the hospital.

"Mum!" I screamed again, while still trying to listen to the Austrian doctor with the funny accent, but still she wouldn't come. "It's Daddy!" I tried again, "He's had an accident. Quick! Come here!" That finally got her going and she stormed out into the hall with a typical, "Why didn't you tell me?" and grabbed the phone from my hand.

"This is Mrs Jones. Who are you and where are you calling from?" The rest of the conversation was pretty one sided, as apart from the occasional, "And what …" or, "But why …" Mum actually kept quiet for once and listened, and the doctor at the other end was obviously on the ball, giving her every piece of information even before she had a chance to ask for it. When she got off the phone she was white - honest, completely white, I'd never seen her that colour and it really scared me. And she was shaking, she couldn't stop. So I helped her back to the dining table and poured her a large brandy - I've seen enough movies to know what to do on such an occasion - and waited for her to speak.

"It's your father," she finally said, after a couple of gulps of the smelly stuff, "He's had an accident."

"Yes I know that, the doctor told me that. Is he all right?" The suspense was literally unbearable, and Mum was at the brandy again. "God Mum, is he all right? Please tell me!"

"Yes, yes, sorry, yes I think so. Well actually he's - no he's fine, he'll be fine." Now my mother is a very successful businesswoman so you'd think she'd be better at lying, but really she's the worst liar in the world, and I could see immediately that she was telling me porkies.

"Look you have to tell me, I have the right to know. I'm old enough and I can take it but you have to tell me - is he all right?" By now I was in hysterics I must admit, and I think Mum knew there was no way she could keep it from me so she took another slug of the Courvoisier and finally came out with:

"He's in intensive care in the hospital - but he's stable," she added quickly when she saw my face. He's had some kind of a fit."

"A fit? What kind of a fit?"

"They don't know exactly. Some kind of a fit or seizure."

"Is it a heart attack? Or a stroke? Is he in a coma? I don't understand, please tell me."

"No, it's not anything like a heart attack. They know that much for sure. But it's too early to tell exactly what it is. We just have to get over there as quickly as possible. So please, I need you to help me, go pack your suitcase, better bring enough clothes for a week anyway, maybe more, I'm going to go online and see can I get a flight tomorrow. Oh I better ring David and Anne and tell them what's happened, he'll want to go over too, won't he? Go on now quick. And don't worry, Dad'll be fine."

"Don't worry," I thought to myself as I threw bundles of clothes into my case, "Everybody's telling me not to worry. How am I supposed not to worry?" Quarter of an hour later I had stuffed most of what I could think of into my suitcase and Mum was up to me.

"Seven twenty tomorrow morning Heathrow to Munich. We'll get the train down to Salzburg. Get to bed now and get some sleep. We have an early start."

"Did you get David and Anne?" Papa had one older brother, an accountant who lived in Fulham with his wife and three children. I liked David, mainly because he reminded me of Papa.

"Yes, they're obviously really upset and worried. David will try and get to Salzburg this week, he's supposed to go to Germany soon anyway on business."

"What about Dobbie and Sirius? And Francis? Hadn't I better get Dorothy to come in again?"

"Good point. Send her a text."

14

Dobbie and Sirius, I should explain, are our cat and dog which we've had a few years. Sirius is a Black Labrador, so really - what else could we have called him? As for Dobbie, he was just so cute when we got him, with his big ears and pointy little nose, and I always loved the house-elf Dobbie, and thought him really cute, so the name seemed to fit. And Francis? Well, if you know "The Half-Blood Prince" you will not need to be told that's our goldfish - he's new of course. They call us the "Harry Potter Generation" but sometimes I think we're more than that. We're a different breed, a new sub-species, Potter is so important to us. He's given us something to believe in and united us - English, Scottish, Welsh, Irish - in a way that never happened before. Harry Potter has changed everything in our lives, changed the way we look at things. Life itself post-HP is different, it's greater, finer, it's more heroic. Just as well - it was looking like I was going to need some of Harry's legendary courage.

Dorothy lives round the corner and she's been minding the pets when we go on holidays since year one. So I sent her a text, apologising for the short notice, but taking another holiday, and could she do another week starting tomorrow. Didn't want to say anything else of course, neighbours you know. Then her reply came and it just cut me up: "Another holiday! Lucky ducks. No problem." God if only she knew!

Then of course I had to text all my friends and tell them I wouldn't be around for the next week. It might even be longer, I had no idea, then I just realised I was supposed to start back in school in two weeks' time. Worry about that later, first my friends. I had tentative plans to meet a couple of them over the coming days, so what was I to say to them? First Penny and horse-riding. Sometimes we ride in the same stables but she has another one she goes to too. I didn't know which one she would be riding in this weekend so it wasn't a problem, I could just tell her I would be away. Then there was Maria who was half expecting me to go into town with her and look at a pair of shoes she wanted in H + M. But nothing definite. Carly was still away, and that left Zoe and Ruth who would be hanging out together anyway. In the end I decided to just send them all the same message: "Called away unexpectedly for a few days. Will be in touch."

That would be enough for everyone except Sally, I'd have to tell her, she's my best friend. We tell each other everything and she's the only one of my friends I could trust to keep something important like this to herself. Ever since the first day we met - which was the first day in the school for both of us - we've been really close.

But since I didn't know anything yet myself, and wouldn't until we got to Austria and to the hospital, there was nothing I could tell her now and nothing I could do except obey the first part of my mother's order and get into bed, but as for sleep, that was impossible. So as I lay awake, in an attempt to take my mind off what had happened to my poor father, I thought instead of Sally, and went back to the very first day we met each other inside the school gates, both of us friendless and completely lost 8-year-olds. Our school is St Cuthbert's in Barnes village which was a short drive for Mum from our house on

Castlenau. I had been deposited by my too-busy-to-come-inside mother, who left me with a: "You know where to go, you've met the teachers and the Principal, so you'll be fine from here, won't you?" Then she gave me a kiss on the cheek, a bit of a hug, and drove off to her important meeting. My Dad couldn't come at all, since he had to start in his own school at exactly the same time as me and there was nothing he could do about that.

Standing a couple of feet inside the school gates I was facing a yard containing the largest gathering of children and teenagers I had ever seen in my life. I turned back round to the gates and the outside world, wondering was there anywhere I could just hide, at least until they'd all gone in, when I saw another poor waif about my size with shaggy fair hair, looking even more scared than me if that was possible, coming in the gates. It was Sally. I remember noticing her uniform was much too big for her as her parents wanted to make it last as long as possible, and we used to have a laugh about that uniform for years afterwards. She had come on her own, having had to walk the mile and a half from what I found out later was her council house in Hammersmith.

We looked at each other, and without exchanging a single word, knew exactly what to do. Side by side we took up our stance, and slowly, steadily, we made our way through the crowd of screaming children up to the front steps and into the school just as the bell started ringing. From there, acting like one entity, a kind of two-headed, four-legged super-schoolgirl, we found our class and sat side by side as the room filled up with noisy and boisterous children until order was imposed by the arrival of a teacher. We had made it, and neither of us could ever break the bond that was forged between us on that formative walk from school-gates to classroom desk.

Everyone in our class had been together already for two years. Sally and I were the only new admissions that year, me because Mum insisted on keeping me in the private Montessori school I'd been in since I was two, believe it or not, as she didn't think I was ready for "big school" yet; Sally because she was a Scholar, and Schols were not admitted before the age of eight. So there we were together, side by side, and it was very much a case of the whole being greater than the sum of the parts. Because we were new the teachers kept asking us stuff to see how much we knew, and because Sally was a Schol and I was the beneficiary of six years of Montessori, the answer was, quite a lot. But if either of us was asked anything we weren't sure of, the other would help, and that way we managed to impress all the teachers and each other. Unfortunately we also managed to antagonise a lot of the rest of the class. This wasn't helped by the first teacher Miss Tierney, a female of advancing years and declining intellect, introducing us as: "Sally Brown who's our only Scholar this year so you can imagine how bright she must be"; and "Judy Jones who has come straight from six years in Montessori". Brilliant!

This elicited the reaction from a certain pretty but unpleasant girl I later identified as Natalie Gorman, that, "I don't think being a *Schol* proves that you're like, *bright*, I think it just proves that you're like, *poor*. And as for the other one, I thought Montessori School was for like, *babies*, I didn't think *anyone* could *possibly* need to stay there until they were like, *eight*! She must be like *really* stupid." That was a bit too much for Miss Tierney to cope with, and she just continued with the lesson.

Then at break time, as Sally and I were sharing our sandwiches and sitting quietly in a corner of the yard, Natalie and her gang surrounded us and politely introduced themselves. "Right you two, *you* - you're a Schol which means you've no money, and *you* - you've spent your life in baby school which means … which means you're a baby. Now, you see us, we're in charge around here coz we're the smartest and we've got the most money, so take a good look at the five of us, and any time you see us in future you get out of our way. Otherwise you'll be sorry."

The rest of the class just kept out of trouble and had their own friends so that, as a consequence of the classroom introduction by one well-meaning but unimaginative teacher Sally and I spent pretty much the whole of our first year in St Cuth's without a single other friend. We didn't care, we had each other and were perfectly happy. As the school was on the Mortlake side of the village we both had to walk in the same direction to get home, both of us going up Castlenau and then Sally continuing up and over the bridge to Hammersmith. So as well as hanging round together in school, we spent lots of time together afterwards, and most days she would drop in to my house for something to eat and maybe do a bit of homework together before she continued on up the road. Six years later we have lots of friends, we still have each other, and

Natalie and her gang are still as obnoxious as on the first day.

All of this went through my mind as I lay awake that night trying desperately not to get too worried about Papa. I think I might have dozed off once or twice before waking up immediately in a panic, and when Mum came into me at around half four, telling me the taxi was due at five, I was wide awake already, and more worried than I had ever been in my life.

We got out to the airport and made the flight with not much time to spare. The plane wasn't full so there were some empty seats at the back where we were, having been among the last to check in. I sat at the window where I always sat, ever since I was a little girl when it was a thrill for me to look out. Mum as usual sat at the aisle (no idea why, she just liked it there), and that left an empty seat between us - Papa's seat. He always sat in the middle and held my hand on take-off; this time I just shut my eyes tight and imagined it. We hadn't had time for breakfast at home so when the stewardess came round with the trolley I ordered my usual ham and cheese toasted Panini and Mum just wanted coffee. If Papa had been there he would have ordered the full breakfast as he always did whenever we got this early morning flight to go on holidays, which was twice a year for the last five years. Then I heard some man in front of me ordering the full breakfast and that was all it took. I suppose I'd been too shocked the previous night to think about what was going on but now it really hit me - the empty seat between us and someone else ordering his favourite breakfast. I just burst into tears and couldn't stop. I mean I literally couldn't stop.

All through the flight Mum kept glaring at me and ordering me under her breath to "for God's sake stop the snivelling". Mum's job title is Chief Executive Officer (meaning she gets to boss everybody around which she loves) and she's used to telling people what to do and having it done immediately and without question. But she didn't seem to realise that you can't just order someone to stop crying when they are more upset than they have ever been in their life. But to give her her due she didn't give up and went on with the whispered threats of death and worse if I didn't turn off the taps. Somehow Mum sounds more threatening the quieter she speaks but this time I didn't care, I was way too far gone. I must have set a new world record for the longest continuous crying fit in an airplane - one for the Guinness Book of Records. I took my book out of my hand luggage and put some music on my iPod, but even the combination of "Harry Potter and the Half-Blood Prince" and Taylor Swift's "Speak Now" couldn't take my mind off what I was going through and stop the tears.

And then the stewardess got all concerned and kept bringing me tissues and asking was I OK and could she do anything or get me anything else. She was so sweet, she nearly ended up in tears herself. "She'll be fine," Mum kept saying, "There's nothing wrong with her; she just needs to pull herself together." Yeah nothing wrong at all, I thought between the sobs, just a fourteen-year-old girl whose whole life has just caved in on her. They say the mother-daughter relationship is hardest during the teenage years, well me and my Mum could write a book on the subject.

We landed at 10.50 local time, and we got off the plane, got our bags, and went down the escalator to the train station, unable to think of anything except where we were going and how to get there. But once we were safely on the right train I sat at the window trying to look at the beautiful Bavarian scenery in the hope it might make me feel something apart from this intense pain deep inside me that I had had ever since I heard the news. You hear the phrase "sick with worry" a lot from grown-ups, but I never knew what it really meant until now. And the closer we got to seeing Dad again the more worried I was, but also in a strange way, the more hopeful I got, feeling sure that if I could just see him and be with him that somehow I could help him to get better again.

A couple of hours later we were opening the door of our little apartment where we left our things, "freshened up", as they say, bought some essentials from the supermarket before it closed, and got ready to face what Mum called "the ordeal". I was just so glad I was going to see Papa and even though the pain and the worry were still there I felt sure if I could just see him everything would be OK.

"Let me have a look at you," Mum ordered as we stood in the little hallway. "Did you brush your hair?"

"Yes. Before we left home."

"That was five hours ago. Get your hairbrush." I went into my bedroom, got the brush and came back and stood in front of the mirror in the hall. As I brushed Mum stood behind me putting on some lipstick. Mum and I don't really look alike except for the eyes - like Harry I look like my father but I have my mother's eyes. She's blonde (well she is now, I think when she was younger it was more brownish - funny how some women's hair goes blonder as they get older) sharp-featured, and tall. I don't think I'll be as tall as her, taking after my Dad who is, let's say, under average height. But I'm not small, a bit less than the class average I suppose, and the rest of me looks OK most of the time. Dark brown hair, Mum's blue eyes, good skin. When we'd both finished doing ourselves up Mum put her arms around me from behind and looked at me in the mirror.

"I don't know what we're going to find when we get to the hospital any more than you do, honey. Let's just hope for the best and, most of all, let's stick together through this difficult time. That's the only way we're going to get through it."

"It's going to be all right, Mum, I know it is," I said, although it was more in hope than expectation.

****

Chapter Two - Papa in Hospital

By the time we reached the hospital they had stabilised Dad's immediate physical condition and they told us he wasn't going to die. It had never occurred to me that he might so that wasn't any great comfort. We met the doctor who had spoken to us on the phone the night before. He was young and good-looking and actually meeting him face-to-face he had pretty good English apart from the letter J issue. He explained that Papa would have to remain in Intensive Care for another week while they monitored his physical progress. As for his mental state it was far too early to even attempt to understand what had happened or to try to treat him. Then he left us, saying he would see if it was possible for us to see Mr Yones now.

"Thank God we have full worldwide medical insurance from the company," Mum remarked to me, "Just imagine the cost of this otherwise." I must have been somehow lacking in imagination at this point in my life as the financial implications of what my poor father was going through were among the last things I could concern myself with. Still, Obedient Daughter that I was, I tried to summon up a picture of the doctor handing Mum a long bill and saying we couldn't have our Dad back until it was paid; that was the kind of thing Papa would have amused me with. No use, it wouldn't come, it just made me want to cry again.

About ten minutes later the doctor returned and brought us with him down a few corridors to the Intensive

Care Unit. As we went he explained to us that we wouldn't be able to go into where Papa was, as it was a 100% sterile environment. I wanted to see Dad, of course, we'd been up half the night, flown a thousand miles or whatever, and taken a train and a taxi to get there as quickly as possible, and I couldn't believe it when they wouldn't let us see him. Not properly, not to be beside him and touch him. All they let us do was stand at this window and look in to where he was lying in a bed that looked more like a cage with all sorts of tubes going in and out of him. God it was awful. Me and Mum just hugged each other and sobbed till they took us away and got us a cup of tea. Then the nice doctor came in to where we were sitting with our tea and sat down beside us. But he had nothing nice to say: "Severely dehydrated, unresponsive to stimuli, seemingly in a catatonic state, inexplicable, too early to predict full recovery," and it went on like that. Most of it I didn't understand or want to, I just wanted to see Papa and give him a hug and that was the one thing I couldn't do. After five minutes the nice doctor with nothing but bad news left us, we finished our tea and got out of there as quickly as we could.

After that there was nothing to do but wait and hope and keep visiting every day to see was there any improvement. So we spent a week walking to and from the hospital which luckily was less than half a mile from the apartment. There's a short cut along a road with some little old houses on it at the foot of the mountain which me and Papa used to climb together. Right at the bottom of the mountain path there's a cemetery and it's so pretty Dad said once when we were passing that he wanted to be buried there (perfect time to be reminded of that!). Then me and Dad used to walk up through the woods and there's a little Gaststube (that's a pub in German) at the top of the mountain and they kept bunnies in a grassy enclosure which we used to feed together. So what with the cemetery and the memories of feeding the bunnies, you can imagine the state I was in every time I arrived at the hospital. I'd controlled the crying at this stage however, so Mum had changed her regular commands to, "Stop sulking for heaven's sake, he'll be fine." But he wasn't fine now, he was in Intensive Care and you don't need a degree from Harvard Medical School to know that they don't put you in there because you're fine. Every day we asked the same question, and every day we received the same polite, friendly and useless reply that he was responding well to treatment. But after a week he was deemed sufficiently recovered physically to be moved to an ordinary ward.

I'll never forget the first day we were allowed in to visit him after he left IC. We were brought in to his six-bed ward by one of the nurses and saw him sitting up in his bed at the far end by the window. He looked perfectly well and seemed to be enjoying the view out over the beautiful grounds and manicured lawns. We both went rushing over to see him, and after the first hugs and tears, when we pulled back to take a look at him, we realized to our horror that though he was looking out the windows, it was at lawns and grounds he saw nothing of, his blank staring eyes seeing nothing at all in this world, nothing in any world for all I knew. Then we tried talking to him, and got absolutely no response. Of course we had been warned what to expect by the doctor but nothing could have prepared us for the reality of the situation.

I suppose we had expected that as soon as Papa was out of danger physically that he would just miraculously wake up and be himself again. Why shouldn't he - isn't that how it always happens in books and movies? But he didn't. I mean he was awake, but not awake if you know what I mean. He wasn't in a coma, but he wasn't there. It wasn't him, just his body; and his mind, his personality, everything that was *him*, was nowhere to be found. Just gone, disappeared, evaporated.

And then things took a turn for what Shakespeare called the tragical-comical. (I have read Hamlet you know.) While in IC I suppose he had been under sedation and had been kept quiet. But now, in the general ward and wide awake, it had started up again - the interesting sound effects that had been heard outside our apartment door by the neighbours and hotel guy. This was the first time that my mother and I and the hospital staff had heard it and all I can say is, although I am only sixteen now as I write this, if I live to be a hundred I know I will never hear any sound ever again that will so chill my heart and freeze the blood in my veins and fill me with such hellish, fiendish terror as the sounds produced by my now-pronounced-physically-healthy, good-as-dead father. Chattering indeed, ape-like indeed. Couldn't be denied. It was the sound of the mad, smelly monkey house in the zoo that we had spent so many happy hours and days in when I was small, now come back to haunt me in the antiseptic, near-silent environment of an

Austrian hospital ward. The doctor and a couple of nurses had come in when they realised what was going on, and they stood beside us. My mother couldn't take the shame and walked out; I met her later outside in the car park physically trembling. Meanwhile I stayed by my father's bed watching and listening while he went on with his obscene cackling, which he occasionally complemented with a further apeing (excuse the pun) of all our evolutionary forebears by sitting up in the bed and performing a kind of rocking motion of his body from the waist up. All that was missing from this inhuman display was the scratching of the armpits and the beating of the chest. I felt a wave of nausea overwhelm me and I thought I was going to be sick. I think that was the most terrifying part of the whole ordeal, when it began to dawn on me that my beloved father, playmate of my childhood, friend of my youth, helper, counsellor, guide to my future, hope of my life, was gone, might be gone forever, and all that was left was this - this moribund relic, this undead, this living corpse, this empty shell, this soulless parody of the great man he had once been, now a chattering, squealing, simian wreck. That was when the floodgates really opened and the boys from Guinness Book of Records started sharpening their pencils.

I felt like I was being sawn in half, right down the middle from top to toe, and half of me was filled with the utmost disgust at what I was seeing, while the other half still loved him because he was still my Dad. And then something almost good happened. As I was just about to rush out and join my mother outside - just to get as far

28

away as possible from this insane thing in front of me - the doctor put his arm around my shoulders in a gesture of the utmost gentleness and kindness, and as we stood there witnessing the complete devastation of a human being, once my father, the abhorrence I was feeling lifted a little, and some of the detached, non-judgmental, infinitely patient, unconditional love of humanity of the professionals beside me passed into me. I looked at my poor demented father and knew what I would do. Whatever it took and for whatever length of time, and however awful it was, I would look after him. And somehow I would find a way to get him out of this terrible state and bring him back to us.

"We will do what we can," said the doctor beside me. "Now you should go to your mother."

$$**************$$

I didn't say anything when I met Mum out in the car park; there was nothing anyone could say. We just walked all the way home in silence and when we got there I retired to my room to check my emails and messages on my little Toshiba laptop ("Tosh" I call him and I never go anywhere without him), while Mum said she was going out. She likes to look around the shops when she's there, or sit and drink coffee in one of the spectacular 19th century cafes famous for their cakes and chocolate. Both of us needed any distraction at all to take our minds off what we had just witnessed.

There was a message from Sally in my Inbox, and I reckoned now would be a good time to tell her what was going on. I have a copy of the IM conversation here and the best thing is if I just copy it out for you. That will give you an idea of what my friend Sally and her family are like. I mean Sally is great, it's just the rest of her family that are a bit of a handful. As I said she's a Schol, and they don't have a lot of money, so she's not like the rest of the girls, which is no bad thing believe me as some of them - God it's just unbelievable the money they have, credit cards, store cards, cash cards, and you should see the rubbish they spend it all on! That's why I like Sally, she's normal. I mean we didn't always live in a big house on Castlenau, so I know what it's like to be normal. But her family are a bit … different I suppose. And I'm not being a snob, I'm not like that at all. It's just that they do take some getting used to.

Sally: Hi. How's things?
Me: Cool, you?
Sally: Me too.
Me: Where are you?
Sally: Just got home from holidays. What's the story - why are you away again? Thought you just got back.
Me: I did, but my Dad's not well so we had to come back over here again.
Sally: Sorry. So you're in Austria again?
Me: Yup, just went into the hospital to see him. First time we saw him he was in intensive care with about 20 tubes sticking into him. Now he's in a ward so I think he's going to be OK.
Sally: That sounds better. Hope he's OK.

Me: Thanks Sal me too. So how was your holiday?

Sally: Disaster as usual. Need you ask?

Me: Why? What happened?

Sally: Do you really want the whole list? How long you got?

Me: All day.

Sally: OK so first Mum she forgets her passport. I mean can you imagine doing that? You see she always keeps her own and Dad hides the others somewhere no one knows where but him. At least he brings them anyway. But Mum, so we get to the airport and we're queuing up you know to check in and suddenly she goes pale and starts checking her handbag and all her other bags and Dad's freaking out saying What? What's the problem? Then he cops on and he's like, Oh you forgot your passport didn't you? And we're nearly at the top of the queue so Dad has to ring his brother who has a key to the house, and he has to go and get the passport and fly out to the airport with it. Only we can't take a chance and wait so Dad and the rest of us check in and go through security and everything and we're waiting to board the plane and they're announcing Mum's name telling her to go to the gate and still no sign of her. Then we finally get on the plane last and we're sitting down waiting to take off convinced that she's not coming when who do you think comes strolling up the aisle like a blushing bride without a care in the world. I had to pretend I didn't know her coz the plane had been delayed and everyone was mad at her. I just wanted to die!!!

Me: Yeah, way embarrassing.

Sally: Then on the coach to the hotel Lucy gets sick all over the place. She always does that in the heat and you'd think we'd know by now and bring some sick bags off the plane or something but no chance.

Me: Poor Lucy, she's a little cutie.

Sally: Not so cute when she's just covered your new trainers in vomit. Then the hotel - more like a block of apartments if you ask me with somewhere to eat and a couple of bars - is a complete dump. I mean God it was awful, they were still building half of it and there was dust everywhere and every morning these guys would start up with their drills right outside our window at seven o'clock! It was unbelievable.

Me: You were where exactly?

Sally: Canaries - Lanza-grotty. So all we do for two weeks is lie by the pool getting covered in dust. I thought I had a great tan after the first day till it all washed off in the shower! Mum and Dad just got drunk every night and embarrassed us at the "family entertainment". I mean it's OK for the young ones, watching their Mum and Dad celebrity-ballroom-dancing or roller-skating (no ice here of course it'd melt) with the Hotel Entertainment Officers but OMG at my age! It was like Butlin's or some place. Then they were riding camels and drinking wine out of jugs with long spouts so the wine went everywhere and playing pass the orange without using your hands - OMG. Cringe! There was one funny thing though. One night we had a "Cowboys and Indians" night - well PC right? So Dad has to put on this Indian head-dress made of feathers and shoot a bow and arrow at a target. Of course he was totally out of it and the head-dress falls down over his face just as he's about to shoot so he misses the target by a mile and the arrow lands on a nearby table full of drinks and breaks every glass and knocks over every bottle. They all went down like skittles. It was hilarious. He was lucky he didn't kill someone.

Me: Did he have to pay for the drinks?

Sally: Naw, the hotel covered for him. They were just glad he hadn't done a General Custer on one of their guests. The holiday wasn't a total waste of time though if you know what I mean …

Me: I can't imagine what …

Sally: I might have met someone. But I gotta go. I'll tell you about it next time maybe if I feel like it. See you.

Me: Bye Sal

Talking to Sally hadn't made me forget where I was or what I was doing there, though she did take my mind off it for a bit, and when we quit I was really lonely and desperately sad. I needed my Papa more than I had ever needed anyone or anything in my life. He'd always been there for me, and I just couldn't bear the pain of not having him. That's when I started praying, something I don't do very often, praying for him to come back, whatever it took, even if it took a miracle. They tell you in convent school to pray every night, but to never ask for a miracle (I suppose they're afraid of antagonising someone up there). Well I didn't care, that's exactly what I was asking for. "Even if it takes a miracle," I prayed, "I don't care, just bring Papa back to me. Bring him back to me."

****

Around this time Dad's brother David arrived, flying into Salzburg one morning from Frankfurt where he had had a meeting the day before. He arrived out to us in a taxi and he was really upset, I'd never seen him like that as he's always really cheery and happy. David looks a lot like Papa, as I said, except he's chubbier and has less hair and looks a bit older. But I'd never seen him looking so worried and it was really scary.

Then Mum and he went to the hospital and I stayed at home in my little room playing cards and listening to music as I so often did. When they came back they both looked a bit shook so I left them alone as they talked together in the living room. We had some lunch together and then David had to get to the airport again to fly back to Frankfurt. As he was leaving Mum said something really strange, and I didn't know if it was supposed to be funny or serious, or just bitter.

"Maybe you can take him to Lourdes with you the next time you go," She said. You see David liked to go to this Pilgrimage town in the south of France every year to help with the handicapped children. He was a Catholic and he went with a local parish group. He didn't expect miracles or anything, he just liked to help the children which was nice. I suppose Dad must have been a Catholic once too but I'd never seen any sign of it.

"I hope I don't have to," David replied seriously, "Let's just hope for the best." And he got into his taxi at the front door and was gone.

Over the next few days the doctors started trying to look at the real problem and its possible causes, though it was far too early to even consider a cure. Papa had been moved to a psychiatric wing which was, disturbingly enough, accessed only by going through some considerable security procedures involving about twenty locked doors (always in pairs - never open another one until the one behind you is locked) and miles of bare corridors. Once we got to him things weren't too bad - the locked doors everywhere had led me to expect to see him in a nice comfy padded cell fetchingly dressed in a strait-jacket - but thankfully he had his own room and seemed to have every possible comfort. After a very brief time in his company when he was quite silent and deceptively like his old self, (the visit was kept brief, I suspected, as the doctors feared another uncontrolled exit by my mother, which would have caused the security people some headaches) we retired to an office where my mother and I were invited to sit down while the Head of the Psychiatric Department, a Professor Meyerhofer, gave us all the information he had, or at least all the information he thought we could handle.

This character was obviously very senior as he had a wizend old face which was all scrunched up, huge big eyes behind thick glasses, and a big head of sparse hair which he pointed at us when we came in, as his face was in his papers. He looked a bit like Gollum's grandfather. I'd never met a psychiatrist before but somehow he fitted my mental picture of what one should look like: an oversized brain in a white coat. But first he surprised us with a joke.

"I haff some gut noos and some bat noos," he said. I couldn't believe my ears. My father's half dead in a mental hospital and this ancient is giving us the doctor-doctor routine.

My brain did a split second run-through of the joke Papa had shared with me - "bad news you've got three months to live good news see that cute nurse over there I've got a date with her tonight". But I was in no mood to hear it again right here and now. Anyway he had moved on.

"Ze gut noos iss the toxicology report iss werry clean. Absolutely nussing showed up (no I'm not going to keep up this German accent thing but you get the idea and you can go on with it yourselves if you like). In fact I haff (last one) never seen such a clean toxicology report. There was not a trace of a single drug in your husband's system. Not even an aspirin. A trance or psychotic episode such as Mr Yones is experiencing quite often has its origins in the abuse of hallucinatory drugs. In such cases, depending on the type, quantity and strength of the drugs involved, the psychosis can be very long-lasting or even permanent. The absence of such a cause makes the case more hopeful of a cure but also more difficult to explain. And that is the bad news. We have a problem treating the condition when we do not understand the cause. Obviously we have ruled out a stroke; there is no sign of any intra-cranial bleeding. You have already stated in your initial interview that Mr Yones had no history of epilepsy, diabetes or any physical conditions that might cause him to enter what we call an acute catatonic trance. That means he has lost all consciousness of the outside world and of his place in it, and has retreated to the farthest and deepest part of his mind where he is now dwelling. It is like the most severe state of autism, and he cannot interact with the outside world."

I was barely listening to all this but at the mention of "autism" I pricked up my ears and blurted out:

"But he *was* autistic! He told me - as a child and teenager - he had, what was it called - Asperger's Syndrome - that's a type of autism isn't it? Remember Mummy, he used to tell us about it."

"Oh he was just imagining it, there was nothing wrong with him."

"On the contrary Mrs Yones, what your daughter is saying may be of great importance. Pray continue little girl."

I felt so chuffed at this that I was willing to overlook the "little girl" comment.

"Well, he used to say that he was bad at communicating, at dealing with people, understanding other people's facial expressions and body language, things like that."

"This is very interesting. Yes, these are all very common symptoms of Asperger's Syndrome. You are obviously a very clever child. Now Miss Yones, there is something else you might be able to help me to understand. Your father, he seems to have regressed into some sort of state of mind where perhaps he thinks he is a monkey and he is imitating the sounds of a monkey or ape. Can you think of any reason what this might be so."

"Oh that's easy."

"It is? This girl is remarkable," Old Gollum said and I beamed. I was now really warming to this strange little fellow so I didn't mind telling him Papa's secrets. It was just Mum I didn't want to know.

"Well you see they called him 'monkey-face' in school - his friends, not the teachers obviously - that was his nickname."

"His 'nickname' you say? What is that?"

"Oh that's a kind of fun name children call each other."

"Ah, ya - *ein Spitzname*. And did he like being called this nickname, this 'monkey-face'?"

"I don't know really. He didn't say, but he probably didn't mind because he liked monkeys, you see monkeys were his favourite animals. Ever since he was a little boy. He always had his birthday parties in the zoo because they lived nearby. Oh, yes, his friends used to change the words of the Happy Birthday song to tease him, he told me. They used to sing: "Happy Birthday to you; You live in the Zoo; You look like a monkey; And you smell like one too.""

"Your father's friends sang that song to him on his Birthday Party?"

"Yes but he didn't mind really."

"Very interesting."

"Oh, and once he was bitten by a monkey but he said it didn't hurt   ."

Again Mum couldn't resist butting in: "How do you know all of this?"

"He talks to me. You know? He tells me things."

38

"Thank you again Mrs Yones, but please to allow your daughter to continue her fascinating story without interruption. Pray tell me exactly what happened."

"Well you see in those days they had a thing called the Chimpanzee's Tea Party at four o' clock every afternoon on the lawn outside the monkey house. And all the chimps would be dressed up in little clothes, dresses for the female chimps and suits and ties for the males, and they'd drink tea and eat cakes and make a mess. And the children could just stand there right beside them and watch them. And sometimes the zookeeper would let a child hold one of the chimpanzees. So when my dad was there for his tenth birthday party (so he told me) they were all at the Chimpanzee's Tea Party and when the zookeeper heard it was his birthday he picked up one of the chimps and gave it to Dad. But he wasn't expecting it and he wasn't ready, and he got a bit of a surprise. Anyway, he must have hurt the chimp somehow because it bit him on the arm, and Papa dropped it and it ran away. Papa started crying of course as his arm was bleeding and when his mother saw the blood she got hysterical and started screaming. Then the other children got scared and everyone went crazy and the chimps went mad, and the zoo keeper was trying to catch the one that ran away and keep the others sitting at the table. Papa said it was hilarious, and he started laughing, and then all the other children started roaring laughing too, and his arm was fine a few hours later. Oh he had to go to the doctor - there was one in the zoo in case of accidents like this - and he got a tetanus jab and he went home with his friends and had the rest of his party at home."

"My dear young lady, this is a very fascinating story you are telling me, and very important informations you are giving. Perhaps it might be the key we are looking for to understanding your father's condition." At this I really got a big head, but I noticed my mother had slumped down in her chair and was in danger of going into her own catatonic trance. Then the doctor turned to her.

"You really have a quite remarkable daughter, Mrs Yones, and the informations she is giving me are excellent. But now I have one important question for you, if you please, and I hope you don't mind me asking you this: Did your husband suffer any memory loss in recent times?"

Now Mum really had a chance to shine: "Memory loss? Are you joking me? He'd forget his head if it wasn't stuck on! He'd forget how to breathe if it didn't happen automatically. He couldn't remember his own name if it wasn't …"

"Mother stop it, that's enough," It was my turn to glare at her for a change.

"Yes, thank you Mrs Yones, I think we can take it that your husband did suffer some loss of memory. How long would you say this had been going on?"

"Since the day he was born?" Mother can be quite biting when she wants.

"But do you think it has been getting worse recently?"

"Oh yes definitely, I have to tell him everything at least three times, he never listens."

"Very interesting, and one more question if you don't mind: Your husband was right-handed was he not?"

40

"Yes he was."

"So I thought. You see, in right handed people the left side of the brain is dominant, so if the left side is damaged or if it shuts down for some other reason, then the right side must take over. Now the right side is where the subconscious lies and when this side is in control the patient may experience severe withdrawal from the world and enter this type of catatonic state, while remaining perfectly functioning physically. This may be what has happened to your husband, although at this stage we cannot be sure. We would like to invite some of our colleagues from other hospitals to examine your husband to see if they have any other opinions, if that is agreeable to you?"

"Examine away, the more the merrier. Do let us know if you discover anything, but now if you don't mind, I really am rather tired and would like to get back to my apartment, so if you wouldn't mind showing myself and my daughter the way out of here I would be very grateful."

"But of course. Just one final question if you please. Is your husband enjoying any particular hobbies?"

"Absolutely none," my mother replied immediately. "He has a couple of obsessions, though."

"Please to explain."

"Well the piano for one. He's good enough to play in a hotel but that's about it. He never made it to the concert stage and never will. But he won't accept that and spends hours thumping away at the thing trying to improve. Then there's the stupid foreign exchange trading. He spends hours every day at that too, staring at these charts on his computer trying to figure out if a squiggly line on the screen is going up or down. I know it's not easy, Forex trading, I have friends who do it and even the professionals get it wrong sometimes, but somehow Jack always seems to get it completely wrong, and has never made a penny out of it since he started. So there you are: one obsession might be enough for most men in the average mid-life crisis but not our Jack - he's got to have two!"

I had been cringing throughout this latest tirade from my darling mother, and wishing to God she would stop, but I noticed Professor Meyerhofer leaning forward over his desk in rapt attention. When she finished he leaned back in his chair and seemed to be thinking deeply.

"But this is most interesting indeed," he said almost to himself. "Yes this is a possibility, we will have to wait and see. Thank you so much for all your informations Mrs Yones, and also to you Miss Yones. Your husband's case is really a most fascinating one."

I could see mother had had all she could take of the inside of a mental hospital, and frankly I was surprised she had lasted that long. So we got up, shook hands with the little old Professor and proceeded down the long corridors and through all the locked double doors like a pair of criminals on day release until we finally got outside into the welcome Austrian sunshine.

We walked home pretty much in silence though I did make the odd effort to cheer us up but it was no use. We went inside and got ourselves something to eat and I just slid into my room quietly and tried to read a book.

Then the IM's started coming in again from Sally. This is how it went:

Sally: You there?

Me: Yup. Hiya.

Sally: How's your Dad?

Me: Not much change. What are you up to?

Sally: Nothing much. Oh I saw Natalie Gorman in Miss Selfridge on Saturday. Buying up the shop with her gold card. Had to go and get sick. Oh yeah I was gonna tell you what happened on holiday.

Me: Hang on let me guess, you met a boy - waiter or guest?

Sally: Judy please, give me a bit of credit.

Me: What was he then?

Sally: Well if you want to know he hired out the windsurfers and pedalos on the beach. And wait for this - he was *eighteen*.

Me: Sally! I don't believe it, and I don't want to hear about it. What happened?

Sally: Oh nothing much, don't sweat it. Though it wasn't for him not trying. He was all over me with his big rough hands. Anyway Mum caught us one night behind his shed on the beach. She'd come looking for me but I don't think she liked what she found. So we had a nice screaming fit in front of Carlos and Mum whacked him across the face with a "She's only *fourteen!!*" that probably put him off me pretty good as the following day I saw him with a much older girl. Reckon he wasn't talking any chances. In a way I was pleased with Mum. He was clearly a scumbag. So after that it was back to babysitting the brats and trying to keep my parents from killing any more guests so I can tell you I was glad to get out of the place.

Me: Poor Sally. I wish you were. We could cheer each other up.

Sally: Me too. In fact I wish I was anywhere except this mad house. It's like living in a lunatic asylum. You couldn't imagine it.

Me: Yeah you're right - couldn't imagine it at all.

****

It was some time before Mum could face the hospital again, despite my entreaties. Meanwhile we had daily bulletins from the medics which showed that they were at least treating my father as a fascinating case. After every head-doctor in the town and region had engaged with him, they got in a couple from Salzburg who poked at the outer borders of his mind with no great success, and when they had left, shaking their heads in bewilderment, I half expected to be given the ominous and iconic information that, "There is only one psychiatrist in all of Europe who may be able to help your father. His methods are to say the least, unorthodox, he has been called a genius by some and a charlatan by others. He is practising in Vienna and his name is Dr Freud." But it didn't come to that. In the end, and with no way of ascertaining any possible cause of his going into catatonic shock, they came to the conclusion that my father had suffered a "sudden, acute onset of a latent or nascent autism, due to causes unknown, but possibly involving reversion to childhood psychological trauma." I know that's a bit of a mouthful but that's what it said on the medical report and I have it right here in my hand.

This was conveyed to us by the same Prof Meyerhofer on our next visit. And as regards any future recovery all we got was polite expressions that' "possibly with sufficient rest and care, he might recover fully his senses", but that there was nothing more they could do for him there in terms of treatment and they must now, regrettably, due to constraints on space, release him to our care.

"Should you wish," the Professor concluded, "There are institutions - or I should say establishments - here in this region of Upper Austria which would care for your husband on a long-time basis. We are all under the same European Union health treaties and you seem to be well insured so there should not be any difficulties securing a place in such an establishment. And, of course as you are having your holiday home here in Austria you would be able to visit your husband whenever you are making your holidays."

I could see mother cringe at the suggestion of such a morbid holiday routine. While all her friends talked of the annual trip to Biarritz or the Maldives, Mum would happily confess to her posh friends: "The usual for me this year, going to the Alps for the fresh air and exercise; oh, and while we're there we might call in to see Jack in his lunatic asylum." I could have told her not to worry though. That wasn't going to happen, there was no way I was going to leave my beloved father in an Austrian mental institution.

"One final question please Professor," said my mother as we were about to leave. How long do you think my husband can be expected to live?"

"It is very difficult to say. We in this hospital have never seen a case quite like this and our colleagues from Salzburg and the other areas likewise have not. So we have no exact experience. However, in most cases of severe autism where the patient is in good physical health and can be well looked after, there is no reason to expect any diminution of the normal life expectancy. Therefore in your husband's case, as he is now fifty-three, I would say he could live another twenty years."

"That long really?"

"Yes, indeed, possibly even longer with some luck," Smiled Prof Meyerhofer.

"Even longer?"

"Yes indeed, maybe another thirty years, with some luck."

"Thirty years."

"Yes, with some luck."

"Some luck," repeated my mother ambiguously.

When we got outside, and all the way home, and for the next three days, however, my mother and I had a certain inability to concur on what was the best thing to do with my father. I wanted to take him home immediately and start getting into a routine which would allow us to look after him. Mother had different ideas.

"Put him in a home," she said. "It's the only place for him, he can't function on his own."

"He doesn't need to, I can help him."

"He's not safe, he's a danger to himself. It's for his own good. And it's what he would have wanted us to do. Remember - he said it himself when mother had the stroke. He said he never wanted to be a burden on anybody. He told us to put him in a home when he got old and incapable."

"He's not old, he's only fifty-three, and he's not incapable. He just needs a little help. He has me."

"You! You're a fourteen-year-old child! What can you do for him? We have to leave him here. How would we get him on a plane? He seems happy here, why can't we leave him? He'll be well looked after, the insurance will pay for it all, he's better off here, really he is!"

"You don't care about Dad at all!" I cried. couldn't believe her attitude.

"Judy really! How could you say such a thing? Of course I care about your father, it's just that I want the best for him."

"No you don't! You're ashamed of him. You're afraid of what all your friends and my friends' mothers will think. All those posh bloody women!"

"Judy really! How dare you …"

"Look Mummy, you do whatever you want, but I'm not going home without him. He's my father and I love him and I'm not ashamed of him like you obviously are. If you want to take a separate plane from us you can and I will go with him on my own, but get this straight: I am not leaving my father in some dreadful asylum for the rest of his life. Anyway you heard the doctor - he will probably recover his senses."

"He said no such thing. He said 'possibly', he said there was a possibility, that's all."

Well a possibility is a possibility and that's good enough for me. That's all I need. What if he came to himself in some awful hospital here and no-one believed that he was recovered, then he might really go mad. It would be like being buried alive."

"Oh you do go on so, there's nothing we can do for him at home. He needs professional help. And of course they will tell us as soon as there is any improvement."

But I couldn't take the chance. Prof Meyerhofer's phrase with its disjointed word order "might recover fully his senses" had firmly implanted itself in my brain, and now it became a kind of mantra to me which I kept repeating to myself, though omitting the conditional "might". "Recover fully his senses … Recover fully his senses …" over and over again I said it: "Recover fully his senses …"

That night I had the strangest dream. I was with Papa, standing in front of him, and he was looking at me and smiling which was wonderful. It was incredible to see him smiling at me again, something I hadn't seen in reality since we had been on holidays together in the summer. But there was something wrong. He was talking but I couldn't hear what he was saying. Then I reached out my hand to touch him and it came up against something cold and hard; there was a thick wall of glass between us. He went on talking to me and smiling just like normal but I couldn't hear him or touch him and I went frantic trying to find a way around the glass wall but it was impossible. I woke up and my face was wet with tears.

****

Chapter Three - Papa on a Plane

In the end the agreement we came to was that Papa would spend a few of days with us in the apartment to see if he could be looked after at home or if he really did need constant medical supervision and would have to go into a home either in Austria or back in England. We wanted to make sure he could perform the necessary basic functions of feeding himself, dressing and washing himself etc, etc. No further details required here for fear of the "too much information" red light flashing. I mean if he was going to be completely dependent then fine, I would agree to the Institution thing but I didn't think he would be and I was delighted over the next few days to be proved right.

From the time we picked him up from the hospital, in fact, he seemed quite changed from the way we had seen him inside. Although he still said nothing he seemed more aware of his surroundings and was generally pretty quiet and well behaved. We had been given a whole bag of medications in case he got unruly, including the ultimate deterrent - a large hypodermic needle pre-armed with a powerful sedative. Little old Professor Meyerhofer came out to the taxi with us which was nice. And as we stood there in the sunshine he said:

"Please to keep in touch and tell me all the news. I will be following Mr Yones's case with extreme interest." He had no idea how true that was going to turn out to be.

My mother sat in the front seat in case the driver needed any help finding his way round the corner to our apartment, and I helped Dad into the back and got in beside him. Just before he closed the door on us, Prof Meyerhofer whispered in my ear: "You have made the right decision my dear, I am very proud of you." That was really nice and made me feel everything would be OK. Then he slipped a card into my hand with the words: "If you ever need any help, young lady, or even just someone to talk to, please to give me a ring."

When we got to the apartment we got Papa settled into the chair he usually sat in. I was worried in case he might have had some bad memories of where he had lost consciousness and kept looking at him for any signs of recognition, good or bad, but there were none. He just sat where he was told and stared off into space, not even out the window at what was really quite a nice view over the garden, with some old 19th Century buildings around it and the mountains in the background. Just off into space. We gave him his dinner which he ate without any problem. Then Mum said, "Do you want to go to the bathroom Jack?" and off he went on his own, remembering where it was. The two of us looked at each other in amazement. Then I had an idea. One of our favourite occupations was watching movies on Tosh, my little 10-inch laptop, so I set it up with the external CD-ROM player and the battery operated speakers and plugged the AC into the wall, and when Papa came back I settled him down beside me on the couch and turned it on. "OK? Ready?" I said, and started the movie. It was one of our favourite Harry Potters, The

Goblet of Fire, and though he seemed to be watching it at first, pretty soon I realised that he was just staring off into space again, and had no interest in Harry, Ron, Hermione and the rest. I don't know why that should have hurt so much but it just tore me apart and I'm afraid I lost it a bit.

"Why won't he watch it?" I started moaning, "He just sits there! Why does he just sit there? He's not even looking at it!" And I'm ashamed to admit it but I starting pulling all the wires and cables out and kept bawling, "What's the point? He's just sitting there, he's not even watching it," till mother came rushing in from the kitchen and stopped me wrecking the place. And of course poor Papa got a fright and started his monkey noises and God what a state everyone got in and I just ran into my bedroom, threw myself down on the bed and roared. I knew I was being a selfish little B but I couldn't help it, I was just in bits. After Mum had got Papa settled she came in and had to hold me real tight till I calmed down and stopped crying. "You poor baby," she said, and I knew I must be in a bad way for her to call me that, "You're not really able for this. I know how much you love your father, and it's a credit to you, but you've no idea what you're letting yourself in for. You're too young to be able to handle this, it's too hard for you emotionally. No-one your age could do it." But thankfully she left it at that and didn't push home her advantage to get me to agree that he had to go back to the hospital. And I know we have our ups and downs to say the least, but as long as I live I'll never forget that time when she could have said, "I told you so" and she didn't. Then she went back to Dad and calmed him down and got him ready for bed. I just got into bed the way I was, didn't even brush my teeth, and sobbed myself to sleep.

The next morning she came in to me first thing and reported that there had been no problems in the night, Papa had even got up once to go to the loo as he usually did, and had found his way there and back in the dark, and had got back into bed and gone to sleep again. I was so pleased.

After breakfast I felt up to another test so I told Mum when she was doing the dishes that I was going to the shops to get a few things and she said, "Fine, see you later." Then I added, "And I'm bringing Papa." She turned around and looked at me. "After last night - do you think that's wise?" And again I was struck by the change in her, that she didn't just immediately say, "No you can't" or "That's stupid" or the kind of things she would have said before. She was asking me, not telling me, and that was such a big step forward in our relationship I couldn't believe it.

"Yes, I think it will be all right," I said. "I promise to look after him, and I won't get upset about anything." So Mum let me go and I remember leaving the apartment building that morning and stepping out into the little narrow street as we had done together so many times, to go to the swimming pool in the summer, or to walk to the bus station to get the bus up to the ski resort in the winter, and I remember thinking, "This is different, this isn't about having fun any more, this is hard, but this is something that is so important for both of us." And we stepped out into the sunshine, holding hands, and crossed the river by the old wrought-iron pedestrian bridge, Papa doing his funny monkey-like walk, with the sun glistening on the water on our right; and the warm breeze felt fresh on my face, and I looked at Papa and I just thought it was so good to be alive. I had never felt that so powerfully ever before in my life.

So we got to the supermarket, got our things and came home, and even a couple of silly teenager girls staring and giggling at us in the supermarket didn't faze me. I just ignored them and found that I could do that quite well and that it worked. A couple of days later we had agreed that we were ready to face the journey home.

****

I am reluctantly going to describe how we got my father home from our small Austrian town and back to Barnes, London SW13. It was a journey I'd rather forget - I know my mother certainly would. The funny thing was, I think my father actually enjoyed the trip, but then he had nothing to worry about. The journey into Salzburg was uneventful, Papa sitting beside me in the back of the taxi, looking out the window and hardly making a sound. I held his hand and looked at him as the beautiful scenery of lakes and mountains flashed by, completely happy that I had him back to myself, and away from the hospital. I couldn't believe that we were going home. It sounds ridiculous that I could have been so happy then; after all, my father was barely alive in any real sense of the word, and I had no clue if he would ever come back to us or how we were going to cope with him. All that mattered was to have him there beside me, and to be going home. I wasn't looking forward to the flight but it just felt so good to be able to look after my own father after so nearly losing him completely that I felt like I could face anything. And I knew that once we got home everything would be all right. Mum could go back to work, we would get someone in to look after Papa during the day and I would be home from school every day at half four to take over. Just getting him out of the hospital, and persuading Mum not to leave him in some mental place, was the greatest achievement. After that anything else would be a piece of cake. Of course getting round Mum hadn't been easy, but if I don't know how to do that by my age I haven't been a very good student at mother-and-daughter school. Anyway I know her, she's all talk and bluster; underneath she has a big heart and knows what the right thing to do is. Sometimes she just needs a bit of a push in the right direction.

So, as the stunningly beautiful Alpine scenery went past completely ignored, I studied my father's face in a way that I had never been able to when he was - before the accident let us say; if I had done he would have immediately made some comment like, "Hey whatcha starin' at? You creepin' me out!" or something like that and we would have had a laugh. But now I could stare all I wanted and he never returned my gaze; ever since the first time we saw him in the hospital he had never once looked at either of us. His eyes were always turned away from us, his gaze staring into space. I had no idea where his mind had gone or what had caused its flight, and I really couldn't try to figure it out. All that could wait. Right now it was enough just to be with him.

As I said he was fifty-three but didn't look it at all. Most people would have said he was no more than forty. No fat, hardly any wrinkles, and a nearly-full head of brown hair. And he was quite handsome in a way when we had the right clothes on him. He must have been handsome fifteen years ago anyway or my beautiful, tall, blonde and ever-so-fussy mother, who could have had any man she wanted for a husband, would never have married him, that's for sure.

So we eventually arrived at Salzburg Airport, Mum pushing the trolley and me holding Dad's hand, which he seemed to like, while he shuffled along in his strange rocking style. The airport was pretty crowded and there was a queue for the check-in which was good as it meant no one noticed Dad's funny walk. And really he didn't look any more confused than most of the other passengers in the place. Don't get me wrong, it's not that I was ashamed or embarrassed about him, I just didn't want people staring at him and pointing at him like the girls in the supermarket - for his sake. I just wanted the three of us to get through the airport like three normal passengers and to get home.

So we did the check-in thing and the security thing without a hitch, except when Dad had to take off his belt and his shoes. He didn't mind at all but unfortunately didn't want to stop at that and when I turned my back for a second he had his shirt off and was working on his trouser buttons before we could stop him. Some people started laughing of course but shut up pretty quickly after Mum glared at them. I was getting quite proud of Mum actually, as once the three of us were together she really became quite defensive of her husband and was ready to annihilate anyone who showed the slightest lack of respect. I had a bit of a job getting him through the X-Ray machine but fortunately the security lady copped on and let me go through with him holding hands. When we reached the Departure Area it was up into the VIP lounge of course, courtesy of Mum's company, and we breathed a sigh of relief. Myself and Dad went up to the snacks and beverages area and I got a packet of biscuits while Papa started stuffing his pockets with everything he could get his hands on. We had a bit of a discussion about that, me and him, and we limited his haul to one each of every bar and packet of sweets on display. Then we went and sat down and he was happy. I was amazed we had made it that far without major incident, as I had no idea how much Dad understood or would follow orders but my optimism was premature as they say, for a few minutes later things took a turn for the worse.

We had gone through the Gate without so much as a second glance from the stewardess and were proceeding down the tunnel when I felt Papa tense up and I knew there would be trouble. But I kept going to the plane door where the usual pair of smiling stewardesses awaited us. That's when he stopped. Just stopped dead, wouldn't budge. I simply couldn't get him to step onto the plane. The pair of stewardesses quickly lost their fixed grins and tried to help but it was no use. They had no clue what they were dealing with and come to that neither had I. There was a bit of a logjam building up behind us so I took Dad aside and started on what had by now become my normal way of speaking to him - rather like the way you would talk to a naughty four-year-old child.

"Now listen Papa," I said firmly but softly, while the other passengers queued up beside us, tactfully ignoring what must, in fairness, have been a rather strange conversation. "This is a plane. It goes up in the air and we fly home in it. It's perfectly safe and nice and comfy. You're going to sit beside me in a nice comfy chair and we'll get lots of nice things to eat." This was the biggest lie of all of course but it seemed to work, that and a Mars bar I pulled out of my pocket and waved in front of him. A few more feet and we were on.

Thanks to Mum we were in the Business Class section right at the front, so at least the "comfy chair" bit was the truth. (This wasn't the normal way we travelled, it has to be said, but she had authorised the additional expense on this occasion considering the circumstances.) We took off without incident and after the usual length of time the cabin crew started coming round with the edibles. And since we were in Business my other promise also came true about the "nice things to eat". Dad ate everything in sight and I began to get the feeling that if he kept this up the lack of fat on him that I told you about would soon become a thing of the past. Then I asked him if he wanted to go to the toilet. We had been through this at home so I knew he would be perfectly fine. I'd say it was nothing more than the slightly cramped size of the airplane toilet that caused what nearly turned into what they call an "air incident". I went up with him while Mum got stuck into some serious air shopping, and everything was fine. I got him into the toilet, showed him where everything was and then backed out pulling the door to. The last thing I said to him was, "Don't lock the door" but the words were hardly out of my mouth when I heard the loud "click" and the little red "occupied" sign appeared on the lock. Oh well, I thought, he'll be able to open it again.

So, what do you think? Any guesses? Anybody think he just slid back the lock two minutes later and we walked back to our seats? Not on your life. Ten minutes later and after a lot of one-sided conversation with the toilet door mainly consisting of the words "slide back the lock" repeated ad nauseam (always wanted to use that phrase) while the stewardess looked on in concern (I seemed to be having that effect on every stewardess I met recently), I heard this really sad sort of whimpering coming from inside. Like a little puppy left alone down in the kitchen on its first night away from its mother. You know the sound? Heartbreaking. But that was just the beginning. First there was the smashing down of the toilet seat a few times. Then the banging on the door. And then (I had been waiting for this but when it came it still broke my heart) - the monkey noises. First just little squeaks and chatters, but then gradually this built up into a crescendo, a symphony, a bravura performance, never before heard outside the confines of Regent's Park Zoo. And certainly never before heard in the Business Class section of an Airbus A320. And as we were right beside the cockpit door it wasn't long before it flew open and out came Biggles, looking like he was half expecting to have to deal with Al Quai'da's finest. By that stage mother had arrived with the paperwork from the Hospital and the Airline's response giving us permission (gee thanks) to bring our Special Needs Passenger along. So that was fine; all we had to do was get a partly deranged and by now completely out-of-control middle-aged man out of a locked toilet. I thought, "brilliant", we've got him this far and now he's going to kill himself in the loo. But I wasn't reckoning with the ingenuity of modern aircraft engineering. Biggles asked us to stand back, had a word with the co-pilot and the door magically sprang open. Apparently there's a switch in the cockpit which activates the toilet lock in case of emergency. Only problem is it seemed to activate every toilet door on the plane as I found out afterwards, and there were a number of passengers caught with their trousers down. Oh well that was their problem and I had problems of my own. Getting Papa out of the tiny compartment and back to his seat was one thing, but getting him to stop the chittering and squeaking was quite another. But finally, with the help of a few more Mars bars and a couple of packets of Wine Gums he calmed down and we made the rest of the journey in relative peace and quiet. Although, now that I think of it, he did rather get the impression that the baggage carrousel was a type of fairground ride and had quite a bit of fun on it before my mother let out a yell - "Jack! Get off that thing immediately" - which could be heard throughout the baggage hall; in fact it probably could have been heard out on the runway above the roar of the planes but it did the trick. By the time we got the baggage and my father off the carrousel and into a taxi we were slightly exhausted you could say. But before long we were back in our lovely home on Castlenau, and as we all sat down with a nice cup of tea, I confidently swore to Mum that, much as I loved him, that was the last time I would ever, ever, *ever* get on a plane with my father. Little did I know!

****

As soon as I had unpacked I had to catch up with all my friends, and especially Sally. So I took out Tosh and went online. Sally was online already as usual so I connected with her and told her all about Dad and how we got him home. Then, with a certain amount of trepidation I asked her if she got home from Lanzarote without any further ado.

Sally: Are you joking me? We can't ever go anywhere by plane without a total disaster. I'm surprised none of my family were on those 9-11 planes, it'd be just the sort of spot of bother we'd get into.

Me: Why? What happened this time? Your Mum forget her passport again?

Sally: No fear - Dad had them all this time, in this really naff purse thing that he bought over there. No, much worse than that, and it was Dad this time. You'd think he'd have known this - I mean he is after all a baggage handler in Heathrow Airport - but he didn't seem to have heard that there's some stuff you can't take in your hand luggage. Like *knives*? *Duh* ! Or like a big bottle of whiskey? I mean *Hello* !! Earth calling employee of British Airways Authority!

Me: Sounds interesting. Go on.

Sally: Yeah, first the knife. You see it was his birthday while we were there so I got him a really nice letter opener coz he's always tearing the bills open and making a mess that guess who has to clear up. It was like a short blade with a lovely handle. What's that stuff they have there, that blue stuff -

Me: Turquoise?

Sally: No the other stuff, Lapis something.

Me; Oh Lapis Lazuli.

Sally: That's the chap. It had this beautiful Lapis Lazuli handle and it was gorgeous. But he just chucked it in his hand luggage and forgot it was there until we got to Security. So we go through and we're collecting our stuff but this big security guard has Dad's bag coz they've spotted something on the X-Ray machine and he wants to know whose it is. I recognise it immediately and think, Oh God, what's he done now?! Then they open it up and not only is my letter-opener in there but they've also pulled out a bottle of whiskey. So Dad's trying to explain that the letter-opener is absolutely *not* a knife and he had no intention of using it to hijack the plane, and he might even have got away with that if it hadn't been for the whiskey. That, he says, is for his nerves because he's afraid of flying. If anybody should be afraid of flying it's me, having to get on planes with that lot. So they confiscate both items and throw them in this big bin they have. Of course as soon as we were gone they'll be taking out the whiskey and having it with their lunch but that was the end of the lovely letter-opener. I was so upset, but of course I couldn't let on.

Not to him, and not in front of the little ones. So I said, "Nice try Dad, thought you'd hijack the plane and get them to take us to Hawaii? Might have had a decent holiday there at least."

Me: Poor Sally.

Sally: Oh he's probably not the worst Dad in the world. I'm sure there's someone out there who's got a worse one.

Me: There's Natalie Gorman's for a start. Have you ever met him? He frightens the life out of me, he's like some kind of reptile. At least your Dad's nice.

Sally: Yeah I suppose his heart's in the right place … it's just a pity about his brain.

Me: Back to school next week. You sorted?

Sally: Not on your life. Haven't even looked at the book-list. In fact thanks for reminding me, better go and do that now. No-one else will. See you.

Me: See you Sal.

I logged off and went to look up my own book-list and to see if Papa was all right. We had our tea and went to bed early as we were all exhausted from the trip. But as soon as I fell asleep I had that same dream again. Papa was standing right in front of me and this time I could clearly see the glass wall, and I realised that he was actually inside one of those big glass cages in the zoo. I looked around me and recognised the inside of the monkey house, full of people staring in the usual fashion at all the monkey and apes, some of them behind bars, the bigger ones, the Orang-Utangs and Gorillas, enclosed by thick glass. And in the middle of it all was Papa in his glass cage looking quite happy and talking away to me but I still couldn't hear a word he was saying. I started looking for a zookeeper and ran madly around asking people to help, pulling at people's arms to try to get them to do something.

"My father's in that cage, help me, get him out - please!" I kept saying to everybody but no-one would listen. Some of them were even looking at him in the cage but they seemed to see nothing wrong or they couldn't even see that he was human. They just ignored him and me completely. I started screaming and woke up in a sweat.

"Papa," I said breathlessly, "Papa, it's OK, I'm going to get you out. I'll get you out somehow, I swear."

****

Chapter Four - Piano Playing Papa

As I had expected, we pretty soon got into a routine. Routine is great; I love routine. Some people think it's boring and prefer what they call spontaneity, which is really just chaos in disguise, but for my money, when you want order in your life, and you want to get things done, give me routine any day.

Auntie Anne had been a nurse before she gave it up to look after her babies and she put us on to an Agency she knew that could provide us with a day nurse for Papa for when I went back to school. Mum had been through half the Agency's list before we found the perfect one. She was a lovely lady by the name of Polly which shows she was of a certain age, as you don't get too many 21-year-old Pollys walking the streets these days I tend to find. She was really sweet, looked really nice with her short wavy silver-blonde hair and big glasses, had every possible qualification you could imagine - she was probably qualified to perform brain surgery if required - and I could see immediately that she knew exactly the right tone and approach to take with Dad. What's more, he could see it too and did everything she said pronto. A couple of weeks later I started back in school again with tons of work to do. Mum was doing her usual nine-to-five (five in the morning that is) and when I came home from school, except when there was hockey practice, I had just enough time to get most of my homework done before Polly clocked out and I had Papa to myself until whatever late hour Mum finally drove the car up the driveway, the lights shining against the curtains telling us she was home.

Those became my favourite moments of the day, when I could look after Papa myself, make his dinner, and Mum's if she was going to be home in time to eat it, and then, in a bizarre reversal of roles from what seemed like only a few years previously, I would play games with him in his bedroom. (Mum had given Dad the best spare room after we got him home, saying he would need his own space and would be better off there.) Apparently, from the age of two, every evening after dinner I would drag my Dad from the dining room as soon as we were finished eating, with the words, "Play in my bed", when I was too young to even know it should be "bedroom". So now I would do the same again, only this time I was the one in charge, and he was the two-year-old, or four-year-old or whatever age his brain had reverted to. And all the games we used to play together when I was little came out again - the Duplo set, the train set, the airport and plastic planes, Don't Wake Up the Dog, Hungry Hippo, My Little Pony, even my Barbie and Bratz dolls for heaven's sake; we played with them all. It wasn't just that the therapists in Austria had said to try and keep him mentally stimulated and that the more one-to-one time spent with him the better his chances of recovery; and it wasn't just that I felt I owed him this as he had done the same for me, spent so much time with me when he could have been watching TV, reading the papers or even playing the piano. The fact is that I enjoyed every minute of it. Then I'd read to him, the exact same picture books, nursery rhymes and stories he had read to me, pointing at the pictures and explaining everything to him. The only difference was I never got any response. But I wasn't giving up. You see I could remember all those books and all the characters in them - like the picture-book alphabet featuring Bossy the Bear and Dilly the Duck and her ducklings - and I could remember every story he told me and the way he told them, making up his own bits every now and then, cracking his jokes, so that I felt that if I repeated everything that he had done, it might trigger something in him and he would come out of it. That's what I prayed for every night that I spent with him, and I suppose that's the real reason why I spent all those hours in his bedroom. So that's where Mum would find us most nights when she finally came home from work; reading and playing on his bedroom floor until we were both exhausted and ready for sleep.

****

And then one day something happened and I got the fright of my life. (Sorry - cliché alert; now where's that ghost of mine?) I came home from school and the first thing I heard when I opened the front door was the sound of very loud piano music. My first thought was, Polly - didn't know Polly could play, she never said anything but then it wouldn't surprise me she's so good at everything. I was still getting the key out of the door as all that passed through my mind. Then as I got further into the hall I realised this was not Polly. No day-nurse from an Agency - no matter if it was Mary Poppins herself - could produce from the piano the extraordinary sounds I was hearing. Must be the radio then or one of Dad's CDs turned up really loud, I thought. I recognised the piece - something by Chopin or Liszt, his two favourites - as I had heard Dad playing his CD of it and trying to play snatches of it himself though he admitted that it was too hard, one of the numerous pieces that he longed to play but which inexplicably, and regardless of how much he practised, remained for him unplayable. Only thing was, it didn't sound like a CD. I went in to the drawing room where we kept the CD Player and quite a large grand piano which Mum had bought for us to replace the old upright when she started making decent money, and the first thing I saw was an entranced Polly perched on the edge of the couch signaling at me to come in but be quiet while she stared in dumb rapture at my father, sitting at the piano and playing like a professional. I had never seen him play like that; in fact I had never seen anyone play like that up close - it was incredible. I thought at first he was cured and had come back to normal, and just happened to have become a concert pianist on the way - unlikely enough in itself and sadly confirmed by his still vacant stare. His fingers and hands were everywhere at once, the speed and the agility were indescribable, at times his fingers were just a blur they moved so fast. And the tone he produced was unlike anything he had every managed in the past. I'm no musical expert I admit, but I knew instinctively that this was good playing; this was the real deal. Not wanting to disturb him, I sat down beside Polly on the couch and she did a funny thing; she took both my hands in hers and squeezed them tight and when she looked at me there were tears in her eyes. This middle-aged, professional paramedic was being moved to tears by what she was hearing. And then I knew that this was the miracle I had been praying for though it wasn't exactly the one I had in mind. But one of my Granny's favourite sayings came to me then, that our prayers are always answered, just not always in the way we expect.

"You didn't tell me your father could play like this," whispered Polly to me.

"He can't," I replied illogically. "I mean, he couldn't, never before, not like this. How long has he been playing?"

"About two hours. And every piece different. He started off just playing some notes, making a noise but not music, just thumping in fact, and I thought, leave him at it if it amuses him to bang away. But then it started to sound different, and got better and better, until he was playing real music, and now this!" And she spread her arm towards the piano and my Dad doing his best Mozart impression. "He's not even looking at any music! It's miraculous!"

And somehow I had to agree with her. It was miraculous. My Dad had performed a miracle. And there was only one phrase that I could think of that absolutely fitted the occasion: "Bloody Hell Harry," I said under my breath.

I'd better explain about my father's piano playing, and first I have to admit that what Mother told the Professor in the hospital was unfortunately pretty much the truth. He'd been playing since he was about 11 or 12 but for whatever reason - sometimes he used to say he didn't start young enough, and sometimes he'd blame bad teaching - he never really reached the level necessary to become a concert pianist, which was all he ever wanted. But being my Dad he never gave up, and spent years and years - his whole life really - desperately trying to improve and reading every book he could find on the subject. He even started writing his own books on piano technique and trying to figure out how it worked and why he couldn't do it properly. Of course everyone he talked to about it, whether they knew anything about piano playing or not, told him the same thing, that the key must be psychological and not physical, and that he'd never become a pianist just by practising, that he had to have the right mental approach. But he didn't believe this and kept on banging away at the thing till he drove himself and everyone else mad.

And now this! Suddenly he was able to play when he had lost all consciousness of himself and the world. So everyone else had been right all along, and it was something psychological that had been holding him back. I immediately thought of Prof Meyerhofer, and decided to ring him as soon as I possibly could to see if that made sense to him.

But first we had to leave Papa at it, as Polly had tidying up to do before she went home, and I had to get stuck into my homework. I thought he was going to play forever but suddenly, at about six o'clock he just stopped and came in for his tea.

"That was beautiful," I said and gave him a big hug. He didn't respond in any way though, and I had to stop myself from getting upset at that, and console myself with the thought of what he had accomplished.

"One miracle at a time Papa! All right?" I said to him. "We'll get there. We'll get you back."

When my mother came home, not too late for once, I went running to her to tell her the great news. "Mum, Mum, guess what, guess what? It's Papa, he can play the piano, he can really play!"

"What are you on about child? I've had a bad day. I thought you were going to tell me something important. I know he can play the piano, he's been playing for years, that's his problem."

"No you don't understand, he can really play now. Not like he used to at all, completely different. He's brilliant. I mean he's like a genius at it now!"

"What are you on about? Look, let me get out of these work things and get me a glass of wine will you? Then we'll have a look at the genius. What's for dinner?"

"Bacon and cabbage. I knew you wouldn't be interested."

"What? You know I don't eat bacon! And as for cabbage!!!"

"Only joking, it's steak. But you have to listen to him. I'll try and get him to play again after dinner. Polly heard him too. She couldn't believe it and was in tears it was so beautiful. He played for two hours before I came home and then for another hour and a half. It was incredible, you should have seen him, he was like a real professional. Really, it's a miracle. Polly even said so."

By this stage Mother was half-way up the stairs, and she turned to me with one of those really serious looks she has, and said, "Now Judy, whatever it was, it wasn't a miracle, so don't go getting your hopes up."

"But it was Mum, it was a miracle, really."

"Judy!" At that I knew when to give up.

So Mum got into what I called her sloppies and I got her dinner on the table as usual and poured her a glass of red wine from the bottle on the sideboard, and I sat there watching her eat and drink. But all I could think of was how to get Dad to play again. He was now sitting in his favourite armchair in the family room staring into an unlit fireplace.

"Will I go and get him now? You're nearly finished and it'll probably take him some time to get him warmed up. Can I, please?

"Oh all right, I don't suppose it will do any harm." That was all the encouragement I needed and dashed into the family room and pretty much dragged my poor Papa out of his comfy chair and into the relative cold of the Drawing Room. Sitting him down at the piano I whispered to him, "Please Papa, play something nice, like you did earlier. Anything at all." Then I retreated to the couch and waited. But of course nothing happened. He just sat there staring off at the far wall, oblivious to the piano in front of him and to my entreaties.

"I can't hear anything," Mother called out in her best sarcastic voice from the dining room. I could happily have strangled her.

"Please Papa. Play something for me, anything at all, like you did earlier. Please Papa." And finally he obliged. He raised his hands over the keys and brought them down with an horrific crash of dissonant noise which caused me to put my hands over my ears but I could still hear mother's yell from the next room, "Judy! What's he doing? Are you all right? Jack stop that noise!"

But once he'd started it seemed like he wanted to go on with his performance and kept banging his fists down on the poor piano keys with the most appalling results. Mum came flying in and took over as I was just about to lose it again.

"Right Judy, go in and clear up. I'll handle this. Jack stop that at once," she yelled at him and grabbed his arms. In fairness to him he seemed to respond quite well to Mother's CEO tone and he submitted without a fight and let her lead him back into the family room and sit him down in his chair. Then she came back to me in the kitchen where I was scrubbing the frying pan to within an inch of its life in a desperate attempt to stop myself from crying. She put her arms around me and hugged me tight, but that only made me want to cry more.

"He did play, he did. I've never heard anything like it. He was amazing. He was just so amazing. The most beautiful music I've ever heard in my life. Oh God!" And I let out a yell of despair. I threw the scrubbing brush into the water, turned around and let Mum hug me, and the two of us stood by the sink and I sobbed.

"He really did play Mum, don't you believe me?"

"Of course I believe you honey, I guess he just didn't want to do it for me."

"But do you think he'll do it again? I mean if he did it once, he can do it again, can't he?"

"Yes of course he can, and I'm sure he will. Where are you going now?"

"I have to make a phone call. Won't take a minute. I'll finish that when I come back."

Although it was late, and even later in Austria being an hour ahead, I just had to see if I could get Prof Meyerhofer. The card he had given me had just one number on it, and he had very kindly added in all the prefixes so I could dial directly from the UK. After I put in all the numbers it gave one funny long beeping sound and then I heard his voice. He'd given me his direct line and I was straight through!

"Meyerhofer."

"Professor Meyerhofer, it's me, Judy Jones." I was so nervous I couldn't think of anything else to say.

"Miss Yones? Really, my young English friend?"

"Yes it's me," I repeated brilliantly, but he was so friendly and I was so happy to hear his voice. "I hope you don't mind me ringing you but I have something really important to tell you."

"Yes my child, please to continue," he said and his funny way of talking reminded me of the hospital which was bad, but also made me realise how far we had all come since those first terrible days, and that gave me the courage to go on. So I told him everything that had happened since we left Austria, right up to that day's triumph and tragedy. When I finished I waited for his response and I almost thought we'd been cut off or I'd bored the poor man to death because there was a bit of a silence at the other end of the line.

"Professor Meyerhofer?" I enquired timidly.

"Yes my dear I am still here, and I am thinking very much of what you have told me. I am not surprised at these newses that your father is playing the piano with brilliance, because I have been thinking something like this might happen. That is why I was asking your mother if Mr Yones was making any hobbies. When she mentioned two things involving music and mathematics, I was very interested. You see most Savant patients who show an extraordinary ability do so in one or other of those two fields. And it seems likely now that this is what your father has become. A Savant is a patient with severe autism who has extraordinary mental or creative powers." Then he went on to explain that with the left side of the brain almost completely shut down, Papa was operating at a subconscious level, and now there were no mental hindrances to his being able to express his musical ability at the piano.

"But why would he not play for me when my mother was there?" I asked.

"Such patients will only do what they feel like doing, and they cannot be made to do something just because you tell them. There has to be the right what we call stimulus. It is very difficult to see what the stimulus is sometimes, and there may be many different ones and they may change from day to day, so it is difficult to know when he will play and when he will not. But one thing is certain: You cannot ever force him to make this performance and it would be very dangerous to try. That is all I can say, Miss Yones, except I congratulate you on all your hard work and all your belief in your father. He would be very proud of you."

These last few words hit a nerve as I could all too easily finish the sentence "… if he was aware of anything in life" and so, as I was afraid I would start crying, I said a very quick thank-you and good-bye to the little old professor and went to see how Papa was. He was in his favourite armchair in the family room as usual, and all I could do was sit on the arm of the chair, put my arm around him and whisper, "You play when you want to Papa. You play when you want to."

I knew by now that nothing was ever going to be easy in this battle, but I was learning to take every little positive bit and cherish it, so when I went to bed that night I did my best to forget the disaster after dinner and kept saying to myself, "He played, he really played, and he'll do it again. I know he will. He'll play again when he wants to."

****

The following day I couldn't wait to get home from school and stood trembling outside the hall door before opening it, trying desperately to hear if there was any piano music coming from inside. But when I opened the door and went in there was silence in the house and my heart fell. I was beginning to wonder if I had imagined it all. Polly was with Dad in the family room giving him his medication.

"Hi Polly, how's Dad?" I asked casually enough.

"Oh he's fine, just fine, I've just finished giving him all his pills."

"Polly?"

"Yes dear?"

"Remember yesterday, when I came home from school?"

"Yes dear?" She turned to me and looked up from her little stool beside Dad's armchair.

"Was Dad playing the piano?"

"Yes dear he was."

"And was he playing it really well? Or just messing about?" I was so nervous I could barely listen to her answer.

"He was playing beautifully, Judy, like a real professional. You weren't just imagining it in case that's what you're worried about."

"Oh thank you, thank you Polly," I cried and gave her a big hug.

"It's just that ... you see I tried to get him to play again last night, when Mummy came home. And he wouldn't. He just made a lot of noise and banged the keys something dreadful. Is that normal, do you think?"

"Perfectly normal my dear, in cases like this. Patients often do something one minute and then absolutely refuse to do it again the next. He might have forgotten he could do it or he might just not have felt like it."

"That's exactly what Professor Meyerhofer said. I forgot to tell you I rang him last night and he said Papa would play only when he feels like it. Oh you're so clever Polly. But if he did do it once, that means he can do it again, if he feels like it, right? I mean, he is capable of playing like that again, isn't he?"

"Yes I suppose he must be if he did it once. The mind is a strange and wonderful thing, Judy, and we really don't understand the half of what goes on in there and how it all works. But quite often when a patient loses conscious awareness of himself, the subconscious mind takes over and they can do things that they weren't able to do before."

"The Professor said that too. What kind of things?"

"Well, some patients become really good at mathematics and can do all sort of complex arithmetic in their heads. And some patients can suddenly paint or draw really well. With your father it seems to be the piano."

"So you think he'll go on playing, when he wants to?"

"Yes my dear. If you want to know what I really think, I believe your father is going to play the piano like that for the rest of his life."

"You know what Polly? You really are a treasure." I gave them both a kiss and went off to do my homework.

Polly's words were so reassuring, and they were all I needed to keep me going, but there was no way I was going to try to get my father to play the piano again, certainly not with my mother in the audience. I would just let him be, and if he felt like it, great. He didn't feel like it for all the next week and I was beginning to think Polly was wrong and he would never, ever play again, when he surprised us all one day when we were least expecting it.

I may have mentioned Mummy's posh friends. Well she's got lots of them. Some of them are bankers, some of them are lawyers, and some of them are just married to bankers and lawyers. Though to be honest some of the minor professions are represented too, and one or two may not even have been to Oxford or Cambridge, including an actual journalist. Those who work outside the home earn vast piles of money and those who don't, earn even more. But all of them are posh. Oh yes, posh with a capital P.O.S.H as the granddad in Chitty Chitty Bang Bang used to sing.

Well I don't know what Mummy was thinking exactly (I rarely do); whether she thought she'd have to get it over with sooner or later, or whether she got a sudden burst of personal humility and family pride, but she decided to invite them all in at once, show them the state Papa was in, let them think whatever they wanted, feel sorry for her or cast her out socially as they saw fit, and then at least it would be over with and she could get on with her life. So she invited them all round for a Sunday morning brunch thing, a kind of Champagne and hash browns do, and myself and Polly were roped in to help. Well - me to help though Mum was quite a good cook and could do everything herself so she really only needed me to do the dirty work of waitressing and clearing up. And Polly was there to look after Papa so they could all see how well Mum looked after Papa.

Anyway, Sunday morning came and after a couple of hours setting the dining room table and writing place cards and arranging flowers (the expression "for crying out loud Mum it's only brunch" may have passed my lips once or twice) we were ready to go. Mum had all the food prepared from the night before so all she had to do was shove everything in the oven at the appropriate time and open a few bottles of bubbly. Now that used to be Papa's job, and very good at it he was too, but needs must and Mum had developed her own method which wasn't exactly what they taught at waitering college and involved simply unwinding the wire and shaking the bottle. She lost a lot of it that way of course, and the kitchen quickly began to resemble the Formula One Grand Prix podium, but it was quicker than all that messing with the cork and it was safer for her nails. She also had a load of red wine of course, and whatever spirits you needed to mix up cocktails for the really hardened drinkers. Then when they were ready to sit down I was to warm up the rolls and the freshly baked home-made supermarket bread and Bob's your uncle.

Dad and Polly were under strict orders to stay in the family room at all times where the guests would be allowed to look in one or two at a time, say hello and disappear again back to the Champagne Cocktails and Bellinis. That way everyone would get the picture with the least amount of explaining to do and the least amount of collateral damage. Dad was all dressed up in his best suit and tie with his newly cut hair neatly combed, and sitting in his chair like that, with the devoted nurse at his side, he really made quite a good impression, which was the desired intention. I was in a new party frock and even Polly had been told to put on her best starched uniform. You can see the way she works, my Mum, and she's really pretty good at it. You have to admire her thoroughness.

At half past twelve there was the first ring at the door and off I went to answer it. It was a woman from Mum's office whom I had met once, and she complemented me on my dress, gave me a kiss on the cheek that missed by about six inches and handed me a bottle and a mink stole. So it went on for the next three quarters of an hour. Answering the door, taking coats and presents, and being incredibly polite to a constant stream of elegant ladies. How they arrived was a matter of intense fascination for me. Some came by taxi, a few drove themselves, a number of them were dropped off by men I assumed to be their husbands though you couldn't be a hundred percent sure about that, and some actually had their own drivers! I couldn't believe it but one or two of these lovelies sat in the back of their long black cars until their liveried and peak-capped chauffeurs actually went round and opened the door for them. I was still staring at the last of these, stepping out of a Rolls-Royce, when I heard "Mouth closed please" behind me and Mum pushed past to greet the lady in question, last to arrive and obviously the Most Important Guest, the wife, as I found out later, of a Government Minister no less. It was like the arrival of the Queen of Sheba, whoever she was. Unfortunately the driver had left her a couple of yards short of our hall door and she was having a bit of trouble with, I imagine, a new pair of high heels, which weren't inter-facing to optimum efficiency with our gravel driveway. So the perfect impression of her arrival in the Rolls was tarnished somewhat by the slightly unsteady few steps to the front door which made her look more like an Essex girl after a good night out rather than the wife of a Government Minister. She could have done with one of those 18th Century sedan chairs to carry her from the car to the house but strangely nobody had thought of that.

Pretty soon they were all safely stowed in the drawing room for a round of pre-drinks drinks, just to get them warmed up, and really nothing could have prepared me for the noise level in that room when the twenty or so of them started yapping at each other at the same time. I didn't mind myself, but I was a bit worried about the effect it might have on poor Papa just down the hall in the family room, so in between serving drinks I kept looking in on himself and Polly to see if he had a couple of cushions over his ears. Surprisingly he was fine and Polly was doing a great job keeping him occupied by getting him to hold out his hands so she could roll up a lot of wool into balls. Strange way to pass the time but it seemed to work.

After about an hour of the ladies impersonating a large tankful of colourful and exotic tropical fish (they obviously believed it was unwise to eat on an empty stomach), Mum gave me the nod, and we started shooing them into the dining room for their eats. At least in there they were further away from Papa, and once they were all sitting in their allotted places, with their Eggs Benedict and

Angels and Devils on Horseback (not a cocktail sausage in sight I can assure you), and a few more crates of Champagne, there was nothing more for me to do until they were gone so I ran for cover to the family room to watch TV with Papa and Polly.

But my retreat didn't last long because pretty soon the door whooshed open and Mum entered.

"I know you've been a great help and I really appreciate it," she said, which made me feel like asking her who *she* was and what she had done with my mother, "But I need you to do just one more job for me please. Can you just go around checking the drinks and see is everyone OK?"

"Do you mean see is there anyone still sober? I don't think so, last I saw them. Only joking, I'm coming."

So I left Polly and Dad together and I'm afraid I must have got a bit distracted because that was when it all started happening again. I was in the dining room with the ladies, and they must have been getting tired of each other at that stage, because when they saw me they couldn't get enough, and for a half an hour they were all over me like fans at a Britney concert, asking me every question you could imagine, about school and my dress mainly, though some of them seemed determined to get me to admit to having the odd boyfriend stashed away. So with all the fuss and all twenty of them talking at me at the same time I nearly didn't hear it. And then all of a sudden I realised what was happening and I'm afraid I let out a bit of a yell: "QUIET PLEASE!" And they all shut up at once, from shock I'd say more than anything else. And then we all heard it, and everyone stayed shut up, and the incredible piano music kept building up, wave upon wave, filling the dining room, filling the whole house, and even though most of these bejeweled Barbie's grannies wouldn't know their Rachmaninovs from their Rimsky-Korsakovs they sat in silence, entranced, looking around at each other and at Mum and me in amazement, eyes wide open, smiles of astonishment on their beautiful faces, because they knew, even through the haze of Bellinis and Turkish cigarettes, that there was something good going on here, and they were listening to something the likes of which they hadn't heard since they were last dragged kicking and screaming to the Wigmore Hall or the Barbican. Then they all, as of one mind, stood up, however unsteadily, as quietly as they could, and tottered into the drawing room where they collapsed into armchairs and sofas or perched on the arms, according to who got there first, and listened, enthralled, to my father playing the piano, Polly looking resplendent in her starched uniform at his side.

I was in shock the whole time and was holding my breath for fear it might all fall apart and Dad would take a look around at his audience and revert to playing with his fists. But he never gave them a glance, just stared off at the opposite wall in a way that for once, considering what he was doing, made him look more artistic than autistic. The ladies were genuinely enjoying the recital but there is a limit to how much real beauty such people can take, so I was wondering how to bring things to a respectable conclusion, and Mum was making frantic signs indicating the same thing was going through her mind, but as Papa showed no sign of stopping, and from our experience of the previous occasion he would probably go on for at least two hours, we both seemed to realise at once that the easiest thing was to clear the room. So the two of us went round everybody, helped them to their feet, woke up one or two who were so overwhelmed by the beauty of the music that they had fallen asleep, and ushered them all back into the dining room.

Well that gave them something to talk about over the coffee and petit fours I can tell you, and suddenly Mum was the centre of attention and everyone was eulogising Papa (if that's the right word) and saying he really should be playing in public with a talent like that and how it must be some kind of miracle that he could suddenly play so incredibly after his "accident" and that's how it all started; that's how the story got about, that a middle-aged man who lived in a perpetual trance, who shuffled around in a kind of bandy-legged stooping gait holding his nurse's hand, who sometimes, it was rumoured, even made monkey noises, could play the piano like one of the greats. And the reason why this story got out was because one of the lovely ladies at my mother's brunch that morning was a highly respected classical music critic with the Sunday Times.

This lady, Henrietta Welch was her name, rang Mum first thing the following morning and asked could she write about Dad without mentioning any real names. Mum didn't see why not, and the following Sunday the article appeared. I have the whole article here - it's in the very first scrapbook - and I will copy some of it out for you. (Of

85

course, being journalism, it's a lot of waffle; a 14-year-old schoolgirl could write better than this):

"In a little corner of suburbia better known for its stockbrokers than its saints, a minor miracle has taken place. No apparitions of eternal religious icons, no cases of the dead arising or the lame walking but a miracle none the less. At the home of a personal friend of mine last Sunday morning I witnessed this miracle. My friend's husband, who for weeks past has been in a catatonic trance, a state as incurable as it is incomprehensible, even to the foremost psychiatric minds in all Austria where it was that he fell ill (and when we're talking Austria, don't forget we're in the very cradle of psychoanalysis, the home of the greats - Sigmund Freud and Karl Jung), a man struck down in the prime of life by a mysterious case of autism, who can barely dress himself and cannot tie his show-laces" - That was an outragious lie, Papa is well able to tie his shoe-laces - *"played three of Franz Liszt's most treacherously difficult works better, I think, than I have ever heard them played. Take the first, "Les jeux d'eau a la Villa d'Este", from the opening trickling, tinkling rivulets building up layer upon layer in a steady crescendo to the cascading cataracts of the middle section, the tone was of an evenness and controlled intensity unsurpassed by any of the great recordings made by the greatest masters of the keyboard over the past fifty years."*

God! she went on like this for another couple of columns and it only gets worse, but honestly I couldn't subject you to any more of it. Phew! But the thing was

86

everybody who read it wanted to know the identity of this mysterious victim of an incurable mental illness who played the piano better than Padarewski. (Don't worry, I've absolutely no clue who on earth this guy was but his name was mentioned in the article.)

The next thing was, these agents who obviously read articles like Ms Welch's all the time looking for new talent, somehow found out our name and number (very mysterious that) and started calling us, wanting to see Papa and hear him play. I suppose like in any walk of life some journalists might find it more difficult to keep a secret than others, and Ms Welch must have let something slip to one of her colleagues who spread it around, but I just wish that Bill had come along at that point to help us fend off this "mob", as we had to do it all ourselves, and it took some doing, believe me. For about a week, every time we picked up the phone (usually Polly or me during the day of course) it was either a journalist looking for an interview or an agent wanting to hear Papa play. In the end Mum had to get back on to her journalist friend Henrietta and plead for help.

So she weeded out the agents down to a friend of hers called Samantha Bleating who could be relied on to be both a good agent and "sensitive to the issues involved" (so she said), and Mum agreed to let her come one day and hear Papa play. And the trick was (let's be honest here, it was a trick, no other word for it) we'd wait till Papa started playing one afternoon and then, because he could probably be relied on to go on playing for at least a couple of hours if left on his own, we'd then ring up this woman Bleating and she'd speed round in her horrible little sports car with her sun glasses on her head and her weird half-baked American accent, and sneak in to listen before Papa stopped. God I hate myself so much just thinking about it again and I don't want to write any more so all I will say is that's exactly what happened, and after that it just sort of snowballed out of control until we were looking at a contract and I felt like that scene in The Godfather (Yes I know I'm too young to have seen the movie, I just read about it OK?) where someone was made an offer he couldn't refuse. I felt like that, like someone had a gun to my head and I had no control over what was happening to Papa any more. I suppose the truth was that half of me wanted it for him, wanted what they were offering him, a list of concerts, tons of money, fame, and I suppose I thought he would want it too if he was able to decide for himself. Also the whole thing felt so unreal that I just went along with it, expecting to wake up any minute and find it had all been a dream (Whopper of a cliché there I know, Ghostie, but please leave it as it's absolutely how I felt).

I'm not going to blame anybody else here and I suppose in the end no harm was done, but I did ask Polly if she thought it was all right, in fact we had some pretty intense discussions on the matter along the lines of:

Me: Are we exploiting him Polly, is this exploitation?

Polly: Not if it's in his own interest, and for his own good, and what he would have wanted, then it cannot be described as exploitation.

Me: But how do we know if it's for his own good? How do we know if it's what he would want?

Polly: How many years did he spend trying to learn how to play the piano properly?

Me: Oh God I don't know, his whole life.

Polly: Right, and if he had been able to play really well, what would he have wanted to do?

Me: I can see what you're getting at but …

Polly: If he had been good enough to play in public, do you think he would have just been happy sitting at home playing on his own?

Me: No of course not. I know, you're right, he would have wanted to play in public. But this is different now.

Polly: How is it different?

Me: Because he is now mentally handicapped, so it's not just a case of someone being good enough to play the piano in public. Now it's completely different. It's a case of someone who is mentally handicapped being good enough to play in public. And that's a completely different matter. You see the public are going to come to see him not because he's a great pianist, or at least not just for that. They're going to come to see him because of his handicap. They'll be gawping at him for the wrong reasons and feeling sorry for him.

Polly: Hang on a minute. Isn't there a female musician who is totally deaf who plays all sorts of what do you call them, percussion instruments, and isn't she the most famous percussion player in the world?

Me: Yes, Evelyn Glennie, we learned about her in school. But …

Polly: Right, so do people come to her concerts to gawp, or because they feel sorry for her? Not at all. They come to hear her play, because she's the best at what she does. It will be the same with your father. She has a disability just like your Dad. There's no difference. Nobody ever suggests that's she's being exploited, do they?

Me: No, and when you put it like that it sounds OK, but there is a difference between them. The difference is exactly what you said. Evelyn Glennie's disability is physical and Dad's is mental, and that's a huge difference. Maybe it shouldn't be, but it is. That's the way people look at mental issues, they're always going to be treated differently.

Polly: You know, for a fourteen-year-old you really are very wise and very mature, and I don't know what else to say to reassure you. You'll just have to go with what your heart tells you.

Me: Thanks Polly.

I decided that was good advice but also thought there was no harm in having a second opinion. So I went straight upstairs to my bedroom, found Prof Meyerhofer's card and rang from the phone in Mum's bedroom. Unlike the ast time there was no answer and I was just about to hang up when the line made a funny click and a woman's voice said something in German. I asked to speak to the Professor but got the devastating answer that he wasn't available and the explanation that he had gone to the United Arab Emirates to treat a "very important private patient" and could not be contacted for at least three weeks. The woman said she would try to pass on a message for me but had to wait for Professor Meyerhofer to ring the Clinic as he could not be disturbed, and she had no idea when that might be. She was very sorry.

Not as sorry as I was when I put down the phone. I knew I was on my own now, and it was a terrible feeling not knowing what to do. I usually have no problem making decisions, or figuring out what's the best thing to do in any set of circumstances, but not now. I knew I could convince Mum one way or the other even if she had a strong opinion on the matter, which I don't think she had. I mean, she probably thought it would be great for Dad, but if I told her it wasn't, I could get her to agree with me. So I was on my own. Help!

****

Chapter Five - Papa Takes to the Stage

In the end Papa decided for us, showing me in the strangest way that it was what he wanted. After the initial performance for Polly there was a gap of about two weeks before the lunching ladies got their thrill. Then he gave it a rest until the day the agent sneaked in after he had started. But that was less than a week later. And after that his performances became more and more frequent until he was playing every single day, for at least two hours and often more. Not only that, but he would actually go and play for anyone who came into the house. Auntie Dolores came one day and as soon as she was in the door Papa got up and toddled off into the drawing room and sat down without even being asked and off he went. Then it got to be an instinctive reaction, that as soon as he heard the doorbell, he was up and off to the piano. It was quite funny really, because even if it was just the postman, or a delivery - any time the doorbell rang or the front door was opened - he was off. And that's what made me feel he was happy playing for people and it was also, 'funnily enough, what gave me the idea of how to get him to go on a stage and play in public.

Now I know some people are not going to like what I am about to describe, and I am really sorry if they don't, but you know from what I've said already that it was such a difficult decision, and I agonised over it and tormented myself night and day over whether what we were doing was right, and fair to him, and in the end we all believed it was, and we became convinced by his own actions that it was exactly what my father himself wanted. I cannot say any more than that.

So what we did to get him on stage was this. The doorbell at home was one of those chime thingies, with two long cylindrical bells hanging from the wall, quite nice they were though a bit old-fashioned, and they made a lovely two-tone ring. They were electric but didn't actually need any wiring, as they sounded exactly the same when hit with a little wooden hammer I found at home. Anyway, as I've said before, that was all Papa needed to get going, so we reckoned if we set up the chimes at the side of whatever stage he was to play on, and we used his own piano every time, then all we needed to do was stand him in the wings where he could see his piano, play the chimes and off he'd go. He was always totally oblivious to anyone else when he played so we just hoped he would remain equally oblivious to a large audience in a concert hall.

The first engagement was in a small recital room off Piccadilly in front of an invited audience including all Mum and Dad's friends, Dad's brother David and his wife Anne and their three children. We drove Papa there, got him dressed up into his tux in the dressing room, and me and Mum stood him at the side of the stage. Polly had come too and she was sitting in the front row of the auditorium. Eight o'clock came, everyone was in their seats, Papa was ready, so I hit the chimes with my little hammer and we waited. He didn't move.

"Go on Papa," I whispered to him, as gently encouraging as I could.

Nothing. I banged the doorbells again.

"Go on Papa, play the piano. Please play the piano. Oh God Mum he won't do it, what will we do?" I whispered frantically.

"Jack!" Mum said as loud as she could without anyone in the audience hearing her. Well actually a little bit louder. Nothing.

I tried one desperate last attempt to get him out on the stage by holding his hand and trying to lead him out. He took a couple of steps and then stopped dead, stood there and started making a few little monkey noises which made me horribly afraid. At that point one or two members of the audience actually started tittering. Right, that was it, I thought, it's over, I'm not putting him through this. We turned round and got back into the wings, but by then Polly, who had seen everything from the front row, was beside us and when Dad saw her he brightened up and let her take his hand. Polly looked at him in the way only Polly can and said one word: "Piano." Then she signalled to me to hit the doorbells again which I obliged with and they were out on the stage before I had time to turn round again. The audience received them "warmly" as they say. I immediately saw what was necessary and ran to find a chair for Polly while she stalled by nodding at the audience shyly while Dad completely ignored them. Luckily I found an old bentwood nearby and flew out onto the stage with it just as Dad was sitting down on the stool. Polly sat beside him and there she stayed for the whole recital. Don't ask me what it was about Polly or why Dad preferred her to either of us, but that was the way it was to be, and for the whole of that recital and for every single one thereafter that was where she sat, to Papa's left and a little behind him, just like a page-turner with no pages to turn.

There was a deathly hush as Papa began to play (Ghostie won't like that). A hushed silence descended on the audience (no, that's not any better). The audience was quiet all right? The first piece was the usual one by Liszt about the waterfalls in some Italian Villa. I had heard it a few times now and was really getting into it. Never thought that would happen to me with classical music. But this piece really does sound like waterfalls and fountains in the sunlight, you wouldn't believe how this guy Franz Liszt does it, you'd really have to hear it, it's amazing. It's kind of hypnotic too in a way, the way the sound builds up, and you're just carried along on these waves of trickling notes - I'm in danger of sounding like that reviewer now so I'd better stop.

When he finished Polly put her hand on his arm to get him to stand up and there was an absolute eruption from the audience. The expression "thunderous applause" comes to mind. The thing was, they didn't just clap politely, they were on their feet stamping and roaring and funnily it seems much louder when you're up on the stage (we were still standing in the wings) than it ever does when you're in the audience, so I'd never heard anything like it. I can see now how actors and performers could get addicted to hearing this, if its directed at them with enough enthusiasm every time they turn up for work. Papa and

Polly took a few funny looking bows which consisted of a kind of curtsey from Polly, and - how can I describe it? - a kind of curtsey from Papa too. Yup, he pretty much just copied what Polly did, and that just made the audience roar all the louder. Then they sat down again at the piano and so, finally, did the audience. Then he went on with his next piece.

And that was the way it was to be, for the rest of that concert and pretty much everyone after it - any of the ones that I saw anyway. Always the same reaction, always the same applause, as if Beethoven or Liszt himself had come back from the grave.

So it was Polly then who managed to choreograph not just Papa's stage entries and exits, but also, after a while, all his breaks between pieces, intermissions, curtain calls and bows. The music she left up to Papa obviously and pretty soon got to know when one piece was finished and got Papa to take a break for applause before going on to the next one. Otherwise he would have just continued for hours playing non-stop. As for the music, it was always the same pieces, which all of us were beginning to recognise and love by now. Always Chopin and Liszt, sometimes a Beethoven Sonata, occasionally something by Rachmaninov. But you see everything he played was well known to the average piano-recital audience and immensely popular, so he was on to a winner from the start. All he had to do was go out on the stage with Polly and play, and he had the audience eating out of his hand (now there's a cliché and a half, let's see Ghostie rewrite that!).

The same journalist friend of Mum's was in the audience that night and again her review in the Sunday Times the following week was ecstatic, and she made a big deal about the "pretty nurse" helping the frail genius on and off the stage. Polly was dead chuffed and blushed like a schoolgirl when we read it to her. The Samantha Bleating agent woman was there too, sitting through the whole concert with her sunglasses on her head (what does she think they are - a hat?), and she reported to us backstage a half an hour later that she already had a series of concerts lined up throughout the UK for my father. Simple as that; but I still disliked her, there was something about her I couldn't put my finger on.

So that's how it all started, Papa's career as a concert pianist. The next one was in the Wigmore Hall a week later, then The Royal Festival Hall a couple of weeks after that, and by then the whole press machine had cranked into action and Papa was a celebrity. Not exactly talk show material as he didn't talk, but they still had him on for the musical items, and that was great because he didn't have to go on or off a stage, he just did his piece on camera, they recorded it and slotted it into the final show when it aired live. And although some of the less salubrious (great word that, it means 'healthy' but it's usually used for 'respectable') specimens of the great British Press Corps started off with the name calling they pretty soon shut up when there was such an outcry against it. Still, they managed to call him Monkey Man once or twice before they were told to stop. It was actually the more "serious" newspapers who came up with the more hurtful comments, and one of them which will remain nameless ran a whole article, not on Dad but obviously as a response to his popularity, on the subject of "The Idiot Savant in History". This purported to be a serious history of people in the past who were geniuses at one thing while not quite being with it in any other aspect of life. People like Kim Peek, speed reader and maths genius - they made a movie about him called Rain Man - and some American twins called Flo and Kay who could do amazing calculations concerning the calendar and concluding of course with my father. In a way those articles were just as hurtful to me as having some idiot (savant or not) in the Sun calling him the Monkey Man. And of course not a word was said against them.

Other articles in the specialist music press like "Piano" magazine made reference to a certain early 20th century pianist by the name of Vladimir de Pachmann who, because of his strange style of sitting at the piano, and constant mutterings to himself, became known as the "Chopinzee". So there was a big long article about de Pachmann, and then at the end the question was posed, was Jack Jones a second "Chopinzee"? Now that's just a sly way of having a dig at the poor man if you ask me, and just as bad as calling him Monkey Man to his face.

Of course the great debate about exploitation was fired up as expected, but at least it was two-sided, as for every pundit who complained that Papa was being exploited, an equal number felt he had as much right to appear on the concert platform as anyone else if his talent justified it. And after me and Mum (and even Polly) had been interviewed a few times and we had all sung off the same hymn sheet and hit them with Polly's "What about Evelyn Glennie you don't say she's being exploited do you?" argument, they took a step back, afraid of being accused of hypocrisy in treating mental health disability differently from physical health issues.

Happily the Mental Health Foundation came down on our side, calling Papa an "ambassador" for mental health patients, welcoming the opening up of an issue people were often afraid to discuss, and praising Papa's and our courage in promoting his great talent and not allowing his disability to hold him back. In fact we met a couple of the leaders of mental health organisations and they were simply the most wonderful people I have ever met. It never ceases to amaze me that the same species of life-form called humanity - homo sapiens sapiens - can contain such completely opposite examples among its members, how it can have examples of pure good and pure evil in the same species. Amazing.

So after the three recitals in London we had to get him ready for a tour of the UK. How we were going to do that no one had the foggiest. Mum obviously couldn't leave her work and I wasn't exactly likely to be let off school. I couldn't quite imagine going to Ms Dunstable our Head, and asking, "May I have the next six weeks off school as my father is doing a concert tour of Great Britain please?" "Of course you may Miss Jones, but do bring me back a program." Oh yes, that would go down exceptionally well at St Cuthbert's.

In the end help came from the most unlikely source. The musical agent Samantha Bleating herself said she would take care of everything. She had all of the dates in all of the theatres around the country booked. This was the itinerary - I have the original letter from the Agent here in the scrapbook: Liverpool Philharmonic Hall; Manchester Hippodrome; The Queen's Hall, Edinburgh; the Royal Concert Hall Glasgow; Birmingham Symphony Hall; Cardiff University Concert Hall - the lot. She did all the organising that needed to be done with them - everything, every detail of every engagement went through her office in the most efficient manner possible. Nothing was overlooked, nothing left to chance and no hint of "it'll be all right on the night". Then she booked all the necessary accommodation in every city and organised a rather large car and driver to take them everywhere, delivering them straight to their hotel, picking them up in time to get to the concert hall, and bringing them back to the hotel afterwards. Then on to the next date in the next city. She had also organised the delivery of our piano to every venue, and having it tuned on arrival. I really had to change my opinion of her after that.

So really there was nothing else anybody needed to do. Dad and Polly were happy together and everything was arranged for them. What more could they want? They didn't even need me to bang the hall doorbells as the agent assured us there would be someone in every venue to do the job. Mum and I would try to catch up with them wherever they were at weekends when we could get out of London and join them in their hotel for a couple of nights. All we had to do was pack up Dad's case - two actually, travelling clothes and concert clothes - making sure he had absolutely everything he might need, and he was ready to face his public. Polly came round and spent the night before they were to leave with us, and I have never seen her so excited. We had already been through an awful lot Polly and us, but this was just the most exciting thing that had ever happened to her in her whole life.

I remember the night before they left, the four of us sitting in the family room after dinner, Papa in his usual armchair, Polly on the little stool beside him, Me and Mum on the two-seater couch, and Polly just couldn't stop talking with excitement. She was talking non-stop about what she had packed and where they were going and all the places they were going to see but mainly about how she couldn't believe it and was it not all a dream, and then something wonderful happened. Papa, who always just sat in whatever chair he was in completely immobile, the only exception being when he was on the piano stool, very slowly reached out his hand from where it lay on the arm of the chair and put it on Polly's. She didn't even notice at first, she was too busy talking, "…and the Manchester Hippodrome - just imagine, I haven't been there since I was a girl when we used to go to the Pantomime every Christmas, and now I'm going to be on the stage …" and then she stopped, noticing we were staring at her.

"Did you see that?" we said, and Polly then realised what had happened and took up Papa's hand and kissed it, the tears pouring down her face. It was so incredible, the first sign of real awareness in Papa, the first real interaction with another person since it started, and maybe even a hint that he could actually come back to us. We all went to bed that night with new hope in our hearts.

So off they went the following morning, Papa and Polly sitting in the back of their long black car, just like a couple of posh lunching ladies, the boot stuffed with their cases. It wasn't a stretch limo or anything tacky like that, just an extra-long Mercedes, and Mum and I waved them off from the hall door as it crunched slowly down the gravel driveway and out the front gate. Of course Mum started crying, and as I brought her back into the house with my arm around her it all came out.

"Who would have thought it?" she said, "Who would have imagined such a thing? I mean, I couldn't have known he would turn out like this, could I? How could anyone have known?" Then she really lost it. "Oh God Judy, I'm such a stupid selfish old woman. I wanted to leave him in a mental home in Austria. It's true, you were right, I was ashamed of him, I didn't want to bring him home, I was afraid of what everybody would think. And now look at him, it's unbelievable ..." and she started really bawling. That's the funny thing about growing up with your mother, I suppose, neither of us has all the answers, we're both struggling to learn how to do it together. So now I got a chance to comfort her and we went and sat down in the family room.

"Now listen Mummy," I said in my best stern but loving voice. "It doesn't matter what you thought over in Austria, you were stressed. What matters is, we did bring him home, both of us, and we've looked after him together. And it was you who organised the lunch when he played the piano and your journalist friend saw him. And that's what started it all. So really it's all thanks to you."

"It is? Really?"

"Yes Mum, so don't be so hard on yourself."

"Yes but now he's gone, and I've probably lost him. You see how he is with Polly, he obviously prefers her company to mine. If he ever comes out of it he'll probably want to leave me and go off with Polly."

"Oh God mother, is that what you're thinking? Is that all you're concerned about? Don't be ridiculous! If that's what you're afraid of then you really *are* a selfish old woman." And I stormed out.

"What? What did I say? Judy!" I could hear her as I went down the hall, but I wasn't listening.

****

It was a couple of weeks before Mum could take enough time from work even at a weekend so we could get to join Dad and Polly. By then they had been up to Edinburgh and Glasgow and had made their way down through the north, and were in the reasonably accessible city of Cardiff. So we packed up on Friday after school and work and drove the three hours along the M4 and into the Welsh capital where we joined them in their extremely comfortable five star hotel. During the drive Mum was silent and I didn't know if she was still hurt or angry at me for what I said, or if she was concerned about how Papa was, or even if she really was worried in case he and Polly had eloped together and they'd never be seen again. After a few attempts at conversation I had to give in and apologise.

"Look Mum," I started off warily, "I'm sorry for what I said. All I meant was there's nothing to worry about, there's no way in a million years Dad would prefer Polly to you. That's just mad, right? Even in a catatonic trance. I mean, Polly's lovely and an absolute treasure and God knows what we would have done without her, we owe her so much. But when Dad comes out of this - and I really believe he will - he's not going to leave you for Polly. That's just not going to happen."

"Really?

"Really."

"And you really do believe he will come out of it?"

"Yes I really do, don't you?"

"I don't know, how can you be so sure? You see I don't understand the difference between just hoping it will happen and believing it will. Obviously I hope he'll come out of it, but I don't know how to believe it."

"Poor Mummy. You've no faith. You don't know how to believe in something." I was genuinely astonished.

"No I don't. I wish I did and I'm sorry, but I don't."

I wanted to explain to her how simple it was to believe in something, but maybe you have to be still half a child to know how it works. It really is easy though, all you have to say is: I believe he will come out of it and be himself again because he's my Papa and I love him more than anything in the world and he's never let me down yet.

****

They had a room each, of course (whether or not Mother half expected them to have moved in together) so we took a twin room on the same floor and surprised them in Papa's room half an hour later. Everyone was ecstatic at the reunion, laughing and crying and even Dad showed some definite interest, much more than I had ever witnessed before. Mum went up to him where he was sitting in a comfy chair by the window, and knelt down in front of him, taking both his hands in hers, and he definitely responded a little, his face definitely brightening up a tiny bit when he saw her. There was a slight movement of the head towards Mum, and the barest flicker of the eyes. It wasn't much and probably no one except us would have noticed it, but it was enough for Mum.

"Did you see that." she cried. "He recognised me, he really did."

"Oh I'm so glad you thought so," agreed Polly. "I'm so glad you can see a change in him. He's been showing little signs like that for a while now. Not much, but little signs of recognition. I really think he's on the mend."

Whether the great psychiatric brains of Vienna and Salzburg would have agreed with a diagnosis that he was "on the mend" I don't know, but it was true for three females in a Cardiff hotel room and that was all that mattered. It was a cause for celebration.

So we left Papa where he was, and the three of us went back to our rooms to - you know, the usual - and an hour later we went down for dinner to this amazing huge dining room full of mirrors and pillars and about a thousand waiting staff. Now, we eat pretty well at home I would say, and we used to get out quite a bit before, but really there's nothing like the grub in a good five star hotel restaurant to make you feel like, "I couldn't care less if I get fat, I could eat like this till I'm twenty stone and be perfectly happy." First there were prawns fried in some oriental spices which tasted like nothing I'd ever eaten before in my life. Then a soup so light and clear you could see right through it to the bottom of the bowl. For the main course I had something to do with a duck, all sorts of vegetables some of which I actually ate, and sliced up creamy potatoes, followed by a huge glass bowl of ice-cream with fruit and chocolate bits and everything on earth to make you go, "WOW!"

Mum and Polly looked at me with shared delight at my enjoyment of the meal, and it occurred to me that with all the worry about Papa since the middle of August which was now three months ago, this was the first time I had really enjoyed eating. And I thought, sometimes it's good just to be a normal teenager. Three hours later we dragged ourselves away from the table, and with serious concerns about whether the lift would cope with the weight of the four of us, we went off to bed.

****

The following night Papa played another concert, this time in a beautiful hall in Cardiff University. We were all so happy going into this lovely hall that night that it was impossible to have imagined how it would end so badly.

The program was the same as usual. We just printed the same programs for the audience everywhere he played, with a note to the effect that, these were the pieces Mr Jones would play although no one knew in which order they would appear. The first piece however was always the Italian Villa fountains one, and as usual when he'd finished he brought the house down (I know, cliché alert, but I'm getting tired of pointing them out for Ghostie, from now on he'll just have to spot them himself). Then he surprised us all by playing the whole three movements (I think they're called) of the Moonlight Sonata. That's by Ludwig van Beethoven, in case anyone's been living under a rock their whole lives. You know the first one is this long, really slow piece in a three-note kind of rhythm with a longer melody note above the other three - oh I can hear it in my head and hum it but I can't describe it in words, I don't think you can do that, it's just not possible. Anyway if you heard it you'd recognise it immediately because it's just the most famous and most beautiful piano piece ever. Bar none. And it makes me cry every single time I hear it. But looking at the audience that night I wasn't the only one. They were all at it, hankies out, dabbing their mascara, even the men, thank God they waited till the end to blow their noses. I could see the whole audience because I stayed on stage in the wings to do my bell banging bit, while Mum sat in the front row. Actually it wasn't really necessary for me to do my Mike Oldfield Tubular Bells impersonation any more as Papa was quite able to go on stage now without it, I just liked to be involved when I could.

After the Beethoven Papa took a break which was a bit earlier than usual but I suppose he just felt like it. Polly said he just got up and hardly even waited for her before leaving the stage. Anyway we thought nothing of it. He went back to his dressing room and the audience got an extra long break in the bar. We did, now that I think about it, have a bit of trouble getting him back on the stage. He just went on sitting there at his mirror with all the light bulbs around it. Yes it's true, they really have those in nearly every theatre dressing room I've been in; I thought it was just something you'd see in movies but they're real.

Eventually we got him back on and he launched into the Chopin Sonata he does, it's the second one with the Funeral March in the middle, in B Flat Minor, it says here on the program in the scrapbook. But you know how the Funeral March goes, everyone does, since it's the most famous funeral march ever and it's trotted out in every cartoon whenever someone gets shot or blown up, and it goes like this really slowly: Dum, Dum, Da-Dum, Dum, Da-Dum, Da-Dum, Da-Dum. Get it? But the first movement of the sonata is really fast, and Papa played it like a demon, faster and louder than I'd ever heard him play it, like he was really mad about something. Then when he came to the Funeral March it was just the most unbearably beautiful and sad music I have ever heard in my life. And I wasn't alone, judging by the number of hankies I was able to see in the audience. Now there is another movement after the Funeral March and that's the end of the Sonata, but Papa just started playing a few bars of it and then suddenly stopped. He's never done that before and poor Polly didn't know what to do. The audience got a bit puzzled too and then he just stood up and started walking off the stage. Polly was too shocked to go with him at first and he was nearly off before she caught up with him and the audience realised what was going on and started applauding. I mean they were as enthusiastic as before but just a bit surprised at the suddenness of the departure. Can't blame them really. But then nothing could induce my father to go back on stage. He just went back to his room and sat there at the mirrored dressing table looking really sad. We tried everything to get him back on stage - he'd only played about half the normal length of time - but nothing worked. In the end the theatre manager had to go on stage and apologise, saying that Mr Jones was not feeling well enough to continue. He offered the audience a refund of half the value of their ticket and you know what - not one single member of the audience, and there were over five hundred of them, not one asked for their money back. I will always be grateful to the people of Cardiff for that.

Mum and Polly and me, we sat in Papa's dressing room for ages that night. We had no choice as we couldn't get him to move, and all the time he just sat there with this look of the most unimaginable sadness on his face. I don't know what it was and of course there was no way of ever finding out, but I think myself it was something to do with the music he played that night and the way he played it. Between the Moonlight Sonata and the Chopin Funeral March, I think it was just too much for him, too emotionally draining. Wouldn't surprise me as it was too much for most people in the audience. Of course Mum had other ideas:

"It's me isn't it? It's because I was there, and I was sitting in the front row. He could see me and I put him off. It's my fault, isn't it?" Of course she didn't believe it was her fault, she just wanted everyone to tell her it wasn't.

"I think you're probably right, Mum," I replied thoughtfully. "I'd say it probably was your fault all right."

"What!? How could you say such a thing? How could it be my fault? I just sat there quietly, he never even looked in my direction."

"All right Mum, have it whichever way you want."

In the end we finally got Papa to come back to the hotel and we put him to bed. Mum went back to her room to nurse her paranoia with a drink and I sat in Polly's room and we looked at each other.

"What do you think it was?" I asked her.

"I've no idea," she replied. "He's never done that before. The problem has always been getting him to stop playing. He's never just stopped himself halfway through a performance. Maybe he's getting tired after all the travelling and performing."

"Maybe that's it. There's probably nothing more to it than that. When's the next concert? Where's that schedule?"

We found the schedule and sat side by side on her bed while we looked at it. There was nothing until the following Wednesday so that made us feel better.

"Polly?" I said. "Remember that conversation we had - about exploitation?"

"Remember it? I think about it every day."

"Are we still doing the right thing?"

She was silent for a long time, just sitting there, looking at me and at the bedspread, while these big tears welled up in her eyes.

"I don't know love," she said as they started rolling down her cheeks, "I don't know. No one's ever done this before. All I know is, he'll tell us himself when he's had enough. But you know, I've sat beside him and listened to him playing for a dozen concerts, and the way he played tonight, I've never heard anything like it in my life. It was like he took all the suffering in the whole world and expressed it through that music. Did you see the audience?"

I nodded, but I couldn't say anything, and we both sat on her bed and cried.

****

There's nothing better than a good night's sleep to make you feel brighter about everything in life, nothing except possibly a Five-Star Hotel buffet breakfast. Now I'm not one of those teenagers who think breakfast is for wimps. I love my breakfast, after all it's the first meal of the day and should be welcomed and treated with respect. Breakfast at home is lovely, but when you come down into the dining room of a great hotel and see everything laid out buffet-style like that it just makes you want to call for the manager and give him a big kiss. I mean there must have been every type of cereal ever created by Mr Kellogg; twenty different flavours of yoghurt; huge glass bowls of fresh fruit salad;

every imaginable fruit juice - even mango and paw-paw; boiled eggs three minutes, boiled eggs ten minutes, poached eggs, scrambled eggs, fried eggs, sunny side up, sunny side down; mushrooms - wild and ordinary; hash browns, flapjacks, waffles; three different types of rashers; four different types of sausages; 27 different relishes, tomatoes grilled or fried; and every conceivable sort of bread and toast. I could have stayed there the whole day. I mean that would have done me for breakfast lunch and dinner, not to mention tea and supper. I'm getting nostalgic just thinking about it. So we all sat together and Mum kept giving out to me for going up to the buffet so often though I did notice that she usually asked me to get her some little thing while I was up. Breakfast at home can be a bit rushed, getting out to school and that, and even at the weekends there always seems to be something to tear off to, so I can safely say this was the first time I ever spent an hour and a half over it. Yum!

****

I went back up to my room and decided I'd better get in touch with Sally again. So I logged on and she was online as usual (she never really does anything else) and this is the way it went:

Me: Hi there, how's it goin?
Sally: Cool. You?

Me: Yeah cool. I'm in this incredible hotel in Cardiff and I've just had the hugest breakfast ever! Don't think I'll need to eat again for a week.

Sally: Great. What ya doin in Cardiff?

Me: Oh my Dad is playing the piano here, so me and Mum came for the weekend. I'll be back in school Monday though. Can't wait (not!). What about you?

Sally: Oh the usual, you know. Nothin much.

Me: Get your homework done?

Sally: Doin it now.

Me: Oh yeah? Looks like it!

Sally: No really, I was online looking up that stuff for History on Wikipedia. You know that stuff about the Romans.

Me: "Roman roads and other signs of Roman civilisation still evident today".

Sally: Yeah, that's it. But who really cares if the Romans were here. I mean, so what? What does it matter? So what if they built really straight roads? It's not like we couldn't have done the same thing a thousand years later if we felt like it, right?

Me: Yes Sally, but I think you're missing the point. The point is that they did build the roads and you can still see them in places today and that's interesting.

Sally: Interesting? Now you're beginning to worry me. Interesting!

Me: Anything wrong Sal?

Sally: That obvious, is it?

Me: Just a tad.

Sally: OK I'll tell you if you promise not to say a word to anyone. Promise!

Me: I promise.

Sally: I think my Dad's having an affair.

Me: What makes you think that?

Sally: Well for one thing, he's really happy all of a sudden, I mean that's not normal for a start. He's always been a miserable old git and that's the way we like it. But now he's goin round the house whistling and even singing sometimes OMG what a racket, and looking really happy. It's freaking me out. And he's always trying to be helpful, you know, like offering to do the dishes, and cutting the grass without being told twenty times. I think Mum's noticed too. Yesterday she said to me had I noticed any change in him. Of course I had to say no and what do you mean but it's so obvious even the babies aren't afraid of him some days. Weird thing is of course, it's impossible. I mean no one in their right mind would want to have an affair with *him*! He's not exactly Johnny Depp now is he? All he does is laze around in his stinking vest all day drinking beer and watching football. Who'd want to have an affair with that? It'd want to be some woman even more disgusting than he is! I wouldn't like to see what *she* looks like! Though now that I think about it even that has changed, I mean he still wears the vest around the house but he bought himself a new suit and now he wears that every time he goes out. It's gross of course, a kind of shiny pin-stripe with too many stripes - yuk!"

Me: It's probably nothing. Maybe he made some money on the horses.

Sally: You joking me? He never does anything but lose. That's why we never have any money - that and the beer and the fags and the football matches with his mates. What a life! I keep having to tell myself, that's why I'm in St Cuthbert's, and that's why I'm gonna stay there and work hard and get to College and get a decent job. So I don't end up like that useless slob.

Me: In that case you better get back to the Romans, hadn't you?

Sally: Yeah, what's that line from Monty Python - "What did the Romans ever do for us?" Maybe they will do something for me. Maybe they'll get me out of this dump. See you Monday Judy.

Me: See you then Sal.

****

Papa and Polly had two more concerts to do in Wales the following week, one on Wednesday and one on Friday, and then they had to do some TV appearances, so we decided it would be better, what with rehearsing and all, if they stayed in Cardiff while Mum and I went home to London. Three weeks later it was all over. They'd been all over the country, Papa had played in all the best concerts halls in England, Scotland and Wales, and they were due home on a Friday at the end of November.

Of course Mum and myself had to have a party ready for the heroes, which meant that Mum said, "We have to have a party ready for the heroes" while I did all the work. I'm not complaining, there's nothing I like better than being able to toddle off to Tesco with a wad of cash and buy anything I want. Which is exactly what I did on Friday afternoon as soon as I got home from school. Then I put up the "Welcome Home" streamers, blew up a few balloons, tying a couple to the gates, and started preparing the food. This time, since I was in charge, we did have cocktail sausages, and mince pies since they were already in the store for Christmas which was only a month away, and mini pizzas, chicken wings and spare ribs - anything that could be done on a tray in the oven in fact - and neither an angel or a devil on horseback in sight. Then to drink I'd bought a couple of 2-litre bottles of Coke and Seven Up, which, along with a couple of large Haagen Daas, made in my opinion for the perfect party. What Mum was going to eat I hadn't really reckoned on, which I know was a bit selfish of me, but then it was Dad's and Polly's party and I was pretty sure there was a steak lurking in the fridge.

Mum got home from work early for once, and after changing her clothes even had time to pour herself a drink before the blaze of headlights and the crunch of fat tyres on our gravel announced the arrival of their big black car. We ran out to greet them, and got Papa into his favourite armchair in the family room before hauling all the cases inside. The driver gave us a hand and we invited him to join us but he politely refused and as he drove his beautiful car out our front gate I stood at the door for a moment just to savour the incredible feeling of complete happiness at having Papa home again. Before going inside to join the party celebrations I looked up to the wintering sky and said a quiet little "Thank-you" to whoever or whatever it was that had answered my prayer all those months ago in Austria and had got Papa this far. "Nearly there," I said, "Just one more little miracle, please, I know you can do it." Then I closed the front door against the chilling winter air and joined the others in the warmth of the fire-lit family room.

What a party we had, and there was no doubt now that Dad was much more aware and more responsive than the last time he had been home. He seemed to know exactly where he was and what was going on, he even managed the odd little smile which was absolutely amazing for us as we'd never seen it before, he just still didn't look at us or talk. But I had an idea.

As soon as we had finished eating and drinking I went off and got something I'd been working on secretly for the past three months - my scrapbooks. I had two filled now with clippings from the newspapers, printed web site pages and our own photos, and I was on to my third. Mum had never seen them as I used to work on them as soon as I came home from school. She and Polly couldn't believe the amount of stuff I had accumulated and Polly kept saying "Oooh look" and "Just imagine" any time she caught sight of a picture or a mention of herself. Then I put the first one down on Papa's lap and went through it with him, pointing out every photo and telling him where it was taken, and showing him the concert programs, advertisements and notices, and reading out all the reviews. And all the time he had this funny little smile on his face which was a joy to see.

"Mum he never used to smile like that before did he?" I asked her just to make sure I wasn't imagining it.

"No darling, you're absolutely right. I haven't seen that before. Polly, when did he start smiling like that, did you notice?"

"Oh that's easy to say, it was exactly the day I told him we were going home."

****

That night I had another dream about Papa, the first in a long time, and I will never forget the feeling, even though I was only dreaming, the mixture of joy at seeing him smile, and terror at the way he was enclosed in the glass cage. But he seemed happy as he smiled and chatted away so I pressed my face right up against the cold, hard glass to try to get as close to him as possible. He was sitting on the ground eating a banana, so like a monkey I just couldn't stop myself from crying. When he was finished the banana he took the skin and started scratching at it with his nails. I was in too bad a state to pay much attention until he suddenly stood up and threw a piece of the banana skin up in the air. To my astonishment it landed at my feet, and it was only then that I realised the cage didn't have a roof and Papa had thrown the banana skin right over the top of the glass wall. Why on earth was another matter, but as I looked at the skin I began to see some marks he had made on the inside. With a bit of effort I was able to read the words, "HI JUDY" scratched with his nail on the soft pith of the inside of the skin. Then another piece came flying

118

over the top and I ran to pick it up. There were only three letters on it - "I L Y". I went back to the glass wall and mouthed the same words back to him over and over again as he faded away and when I woke up I was still saying, "I love you".

****

Chapter Six - Papa Goes on a Concert Tour of Europe

"The reason I like 'The Half-Blood Prince' so much is because it's all about love. Harry doesn't have to fight any dragons, or survive a confrontation with Voldemort, or even solve any great mysteries. It's a kind of oasis of calm in the middle of all the turmoil in their lives. Hermione realizes she really loves Ron when he is seduced by Lavender; Harry nearly falls victim to an Amortentia Love Potion sent to him by Romilda Vane in a box of chocolates; Ron realises its Hermione he really loves when, unconscious on his hospital bed after being poisoned, he calls out her name; and of course Harry and Ginny have their first kiss and fall in love. They all get a little bit of happiness and normality in their otherwise terrifying lives. I know I'm only fourteen, but I've a feeling that that's what life is all about. If you can snatch a little bit of love and happiness in the middle of all the chaos and the struggle then you're doing pretty well. For me, so far in my life, that love and happiness has come from my Papa. (I know Mum loves me too and of course I love her but it's different.) Later on there will be boys and then hopefully the whole marriage-and-living-happily-ever-after bit, and children, little bits of me and him running around, boy will that be weird! But right now I just want to look after my Papa and give him back some of the love and caring that he gave me

all my life. Then maybe my miracle will happen and he'll come back to me."

I don't ever let anybody see my diary *ever* but I thought I should just copy out that short entry from the day Papa came home because it really shows what was going through my head at the time.

The next thing that sticks out in my mind from the whirlwind that our lives became around then was a visit from the lady in the sports car, Ms Bleating, looking splendid in a little Chanel-style black suit, and even though it was a month before Christmas where do you think she had the sunglasses? Yup you guessed it - on her head. Maybe the hair's really a wig, I thought, and she needs the sunglasses there to keep it in place. Anyway you know the expression not to "let the grass grow under your feet", well that's a cliché that no one is ever going to be even mildly tempted to use against our Ms Bleating. I mean Papa and Polly hadn't even been home a day from a long and tiring tour of GB when she turns up on the doorstep with a list of engagements all over Europe as long as her arm. We all sat down around the dining table while she read it off in her mock-New York accent which still persisted in getting on my nerves, her red-and-white-framed reading glasses making a lovely contrast to the sunglasses still on the top of her head. A six-month tour of twelve European countries starting in the New Year and including every major city in Europe. Everywhere from Cork to Constantinople; Valentia to Vladivostok. I'm exaggerating slightly, I just got those names from my school atlas, but it was a long list, I have it here in the scrapbook.

They were to start in Ireland, Dublin and Cork, then get the ferry down to Spain and Portugal, then round by the South of France to Italy, up through Austria (including Salzburg so that would be interesting to say the least), Germany, the three Scandinavian countries, and back down through Denmark, Holland and France and then home. Again they were going to travel in the same huge luxury car, since it was the easiest way to get both of them and all their bags around. All Papa and Polly had to do was get into the car and relax. Compared with flying, or going by train and having to get taxis between airports or train stations and hotels, it was so much easier. OK there was an awful lot of driving but sitting still was what Papa did best, and there was no walking or standing around or queuing up - perfect! I still didn't like this Bleating woman, but I had to admire her organisational ability and I was being taught a lesson in not judging people on appearance. But in spite of the efficiency of the arrangements there was still a major doubt in my mind as to whether Papa would be up to it all.

"What do you think, Mum?" I asked after we'd told the agent we'd obviously have to think about it and she'd gone off in her noisy two-seater.

"I really couldn't say, Polly is probably the person best qualified to advise us." Maybe I was imagining it but I thought I caught a hint of sniffiness in my mother's tone of voice.

"Well Polly?" I asked the person best qualified to advise us. "First of all, are *you* up to it?"

"Oh don't worry about me, That's no problem at all. I enjoy travelling and all I have to do is sit there on the stage."

"What about Papa then, what do you think?"

"Tell you what, why don't we ask him."

"Polly?" I was beginning to wonder if the strain had been too much for our wonderful nurse. "What are you saying Polly?" I enquired hesitantly.

"It's all right Judy, you don't need to look at me like that, I haven't gone completely loopy. Just follow me, you too Jenny. And bring that schedule."

Out of curiosity as much as a desire to please, me and Mum did as we were told, and followed Polly into the family room where Papa sat in his usual armchair in front of the fire, staring blankly into the flames.

"Right, now give me that list of cities. Listen Jack, after Christmas we're going to play some more concerts all right?" There was no reaction whatsoever but Polly went on: "We're going to play in all these cities - now listen." Then she started on the list of European capitals that we hoped they would visit.

"Dublin … Cork … Santander … Lisbon … Madrid … Barcelona …" At that point me and Mum noticed a definite sign of interest or recognition coming into Dad's expression; we both looked at each other and nodded. But Polly was going on with the list: "… Monaco … Milan … Florence … Rome … Venice … Geneva … Zurich …" (by this point Papa's face had resumed the smile we'd seen the previous night and we thought we were on to a winner, until the very next name on the list wiped it out) "…

Salzburg ... Vien-" But Polly had no chance to finish the name of Austria's capital because at the mention of the birthplace of the great Wolfgang Amadeus Mozart my poor Papa had lost the smile and immediately started up a ferocious barrage of chimp noises. I hadn't heard them for so long that it was a real shock and quite frightening for all of us in that small room. Mum and myself looked at each other in dismay, Mum actually putting her hands over her ears. I couldn't blame her, the screeching was so loud and upsetting. I didn't know what to do but Polly was immediately in control of the situation.

"OK Jack no Salzburg. Do you hear, no Salzburg - all right?" And the chattering died down almost immediately to just the odd little squeak. Then Polly was off again.

"Vienna - how about Vienna? OK?" Squeak - squeak - squeak!" "OK no Vienna, off the list, no Austria at all OK?" Squeak. "What about Munich? Munich all right? OK ... Dusseldorf ... Cologne ... Bonn ... Copenhagen ..." But there was no more trouble and by the time she got to Stockholm there was a real smile on Papa's face. The last concert was in Paris after which they and the car were to get on the Eurostar for London. Arriving in Waterloo late at night they could be home in Barnes in half an hour easy. By the time Polly was finished she had pretty much convinced all of us that it was possible. Mother was looking at the three of us with a look of complete amazement on her face, I gave Polly the biggest hug ever, and by his standards Papa was practically grinning! I've said it before and I'll probably say it again: what a treasure Polly is!

But before any of the European Tour was to commence we had the small detail of Christmas to negotiate. And what a Christmas it was going to be. What could have been a scene of tragedy with myself and my mother doing our best to put on a brave face with a severely mentally challenged father to look after, had become, as a result of the extraordinary events of the previous four months, an occasion of real celebration and hope. So much so that Mum succumbed to an excess of festive cheer and invited her two brothers and their families round for drinks on Christmas morning. Now I know I haven't mentioned Mum's family up until now and there's a very good reason for that: she never mentions them herself. Really - it's as if they didn't exist. Just exactly why I had never been given a clue, but maybe I was about to find out. I supposed it was Mummy's tendency to reject people who didn't match up to the extremely high standards of perfection necessary to meet with her ongoing approval that had caused the family rift, but as it turned out, and to my shame, I was completely wrong.

The run-up to Christmas was the usual hectic (I think is the accepted word) affair. We finished up in school on the Friday before, the 19th I think it was, and that was the perennial mixture of relief at getting another term over and highly emotional partings from all our best and dearest friends, some of whom we would never ever see again for the next two weeks.

Just before we broke up, however, we had the mandatory end-of-term exams and something very unusual happened at one of them. I've mentioned Natalie Gorman, one of the sweetest, kindest girls in my class. Now Natalie's also a very generous girl, giving everyone in the class an opportunity to envy her - those who don't envy her for her looks can be jealous of her brains because she has both, oh yes, believe me, she has both in bucket-fulls (or should that be buckets-full?) You would think that just by the law of averages or something mathematical, no one could be as good-looking and as clever as she is, but there she is, living proof of what it says in the Bible: "To those who have, more shall be given." Add to those bounteous gifts of God or Nature a father who is "in the very high sevens" - meaning he earns a seven-figure sum, over one million pounds per annum (that's what they say to each other that lot, they won't let anyone into their gang unless their father is "in the sevens". I mean, can you believe it?!) - and the result would look like she's pretty much set up for life. In fact her life looks so predictably perfect it must be hardly worth living.

So what, you might ask, would make a girl like that cheat at an end-of-term Maths test? Yes you read correctly. She cheated at the Maths test and she got caught! Some less restrained girls were reported to have let out whoops of joy on hearing the news but that's not confirmed. This is what happened in the exam anyway and I saw it all myself.

We're all in 3A and B for the test - they've opened up the partition to make one big room and I'm near the back of B so I can see everyone in both classrooms. I'm also pretty good at Maths so I got finished early and I'm just checking through the paper when I see something you don't often see. Natalie's desk is at the sliding doors just inside 3B and up against the right-hand partition so there's a bit to her right that the supervisor Mr Dodds our maths teacher cannot see. And she's got all these notes in her right hand that she's holding up just behind the partition and out of sight of Dodds, but everyone sitting behind Natalie can see exactly what she's doing. You can see why too. Of course she doesn't need to cog - Maths is one of her best subjects and she never gets anything less than an A+. She was just showing off, that and of course daring any of us to give her away. Any one of us could have done it - just put up our hand and said, "Excuse me Sir, but Natalie is cheating," Dodds would have come down, found Natalie's notes which she had nowhere to conceal, and that would have been that. It was the simplest thing in the world for any of us to give her away, and that was the pleasure she got from it. She knew we couldn't do a thing about it. Anyone who would have dared to peach would never have had a friend left in the school. They would have been an outcast, friendless, alone. The city of Coventry comes to mind. So what Natalie was really doing was to remind us of that fact, while exercising her power over us, and showing us how reckless of authority she could be. It was a brilliant performance in its daring and cunning, and I almost had to admire her for it. Unfortunately she hadn't reckoned with the superior observant powers of Mr Jeremiah B. Dodds. He, noticing the faint but perceptible flurry of attention being drawn towards the corner by the dividing doors

127

where Ms Gorman was sitting, instead of going straight down the classroom, which would have given those concerned time to cover up, he silently slipped out of his door, in 3 A, came down the corridor and equally silently opened the door of 3 B, thus arriving in beside me and behind Natalie from where he caught a perfect sight of her demonstration of bravura in waving her cog-notes in her hand. Creeping up behind her, he snatched them out of her hand with a "I'll take those Miss Gorman" and was back up to the top of the class before Natalie could even understand how he had done it. I tell you I witnessed the whole event and it was first rate entertainment. Better than any mime ever thought up in Drama class.

"You're for it," said Annie Ferry afterwards, not one of Natalie's greatest admirers, "That'll mean expulsion and good riddance I say." She was right too, cheating at an exam did carry only one punishment, instant dismissal from the school. Natalie was characteristically brazen however.

"You wish, Ferry, and you'll be sorry you said that. Think they'd expel me? Fat chance - they wouldn't dare."

I wouldn't have liked to put money on it either way, knowing the Gorman family and the influence their money can buy, and anyway it was the last day of school and nothing was going to happen until the new term. Might do Natalie some good, I thought, having to sweat over the possible consequences of her actions until after Christmas. Didn't bother me anyway, I was just happy to get home that day knowing I was free until the first week in January. When I got home I couldn't believe my eyes - or my nose.

Mum was in the kitchen up to her elbows in a big bowl of Christmas cake mix which she was kneading by hand! I hadn't seen her doing that since I was about eight, and the sight and the overwhelming smell of the ingredients instantly brought me back to my childhood when every year at this time I would "help Mummy make the cake".

"Mum? Are you all right? Why aren't you at work? You haven't been fired have you?"

"Don't be silly Judy, can't I make a Christmas cake if I feel like it?"

"Of course, it's lovely, but you haven't made one yourself in about five or six years, and it is four o'clock on a Friday afternoon which for you is the middle of the work-day."

"Not today. Today I wanted to be with my family."

"I think you really should go have a lie down now."

"Now stop it Judy, stop trying to be smart, you know I don't like it. As it happens I was sitting in the office looking at a pile of work and I said to myself, 'Does this really have to be done now?' And I thought about it and realised it could easily wait until after Christmas. Then it occurred to me what day it was - the Friday before Christmas - and what we always used to do on this day, so I thought I'd just come home and surprise you and get started. So here I am."

"Wow!"

"That's all you can say - 'Wow'?"

"Yeah, that's about it - Wow! Oh and … you've got some flour on your nose … just there …"

I rubbed off the flour and asked her could I help and pretty soon it was just like old times again, the two of us chucking raisins and sultanas into the weighing scales and mixing up spices in mortars, and while we worked I told her the incredible-but-true story of Natalie and kept thinking how lucky I was really. I had a great Mum who loved me and looked after me, and who earned a salary which, though it certainly wasn't "in the sevens" was absolutely enough for us. I also had the opportunity of looking after my Dad and maybe, with a bit of luck, seeing him eventually recover. And with Christmas just round the corner and my birthday two days before that, what more could a soon-to-be-15-year-old want in life? Nothing!

Birthdays are funny things; for the first ten or twelve of them your Mum and Dad make a big fuss and make it the best day of the year bar Christmas Day. And don't get me wrong, you're very grateful to them for it. But then you get to my age and all you want to do is hang out with your friends, go to a movie, get a pizza and just chill. So that's exactly what we did this year and it was the best. We ended up at home in my room listening to music and having a laugh. All my mates were there, Penny and Maria and Zoe and Ruth and Carly, and of course Sally. We'd been to see "The Deathly Hallows" again - my third time seeing it - and between that and my story of how the mighty Natalie got her come-uppance, we had plenty to talk about.

****

Christmas morning - what can I say? Everyone has their own perfect idea of Christmas - either a memory or (if they're young enough) reality. Going to church, opening presents, whatever it might involve, but for everyone it's always perfect, the best day of the year which absolutely nothing can spoil. Unless your mother has invited her weird brothers with their weird wives and weirder children (my cousins - help!) to come to your house for drinks!

For reasons which pretty soon became clear, Papa had been left over to Polly's flat in Islington in the morning and he was to stay there till after lunch. She lived on her own and didn't have any family near enough to spend Christmas with so she was absolutely delighted to have Papa there with her for a few hours. Mum had arranged to pick him up at about three - or maybe after the Queen's Christmas message. I couldn't wait to get rid of the relations and get to spend the rest of Christmas Day with my Papa, but first we had to be polite and on our best behaviour according to Mum - as it turned out it's a pity she didn't tell our guests the same thing.

I had a bad feeling about it from the start, and had no idea why Mum was doing this, and my feeling just got worse when I saw the two families drive in the gates in their big Japanese 4WD things. Firstly they all arrived together - or at least at the same time - so I never figured out which brother was with which wife and children. But it probably didn't really matter as they were pretty much interchangeable. The two brothers looked remarkably alike, with their short cropped hair and heavy build, but more remarkably they looked absolutely nothing like my mother.

Nor did they sound like her, having distinct Northern accents.

I was introduced to them, I must admit, as Uncle George and Auntie Maggie and Uncle Philip and Auntie Grace but I quickly lost track of who was who when it came to all the cousins. There must have been about ten of these - I don't think Mum could have had a full up-to-date list of all her nieces and nephews when she had the idea of inviting them. Anyway, she had enough presents for everyone, having gone way over the top in Hamleys the week before, and bought everything she saw 'just in case'. Funny thing was, I didn't get anything from any of the relations. Now I don't mind, and I didn't expect anything of course, I mean I don't even know these people really. It's just a bit odd, that they'd come for drinks on Christmas morning and not bring a present, you know? Also their clothes struck me as a bit strange. Now I don't want to sound petty or superficial, but most people do believe in making a bit of an effort in the clothes department for Christmas Day. I mean it's just one day in the year when I think it's important to try to look your best. I know true beauty is on the inside but it doesn't hurt to wear something nice occasionally, especially on Christmas morning. Mum's brothers obviously didn't see it like that, as one of them was in a T-shirt and dirty old jeans, and the other was in a hoodie and dirty old jeans. Smooth.

OK the wives had made a bit of an effort though Mum and I agreed afterwards it might have been better if they hadn't. I know you're going to think we're being bitchy but really you should have seen this pair. They looked like a couple of overweight Stringfellow's employees on a night off. Don't ask how I know about Mr Stringfellow, I may go to a Convent School but that doesn't mean I live in a Convent.

But it was the children that really gave me cause to reconsider my family ties. These are the ones I managed to make mental notes on: one pair of twins, male, age about six, dressed in combat fatigues, armed with convincing replica Uzi sub-machine guns which produced very authentic sound effects, spent the whole two hours running uncontrollably around the house firing their Uzis at anything that moved; one male, age ten, weight at least twelve stone, dressed in something loose, spent the entire time at the dining table stuffing himself with everything he could lay his hands on; one female, age about nine, same size, same weight, same clothing, same interest in comestibles, might be his sister; one male, age eight or nine, chased Dobbie around the garden in an attempt to empty the contents of a watering can over him; a second pair of twins, female, age 12, spent the entire time sneaking round the bedrooms - in the end I had to lock mine and remove the key after I found them in there, nosing through my personal belongings and lying on my bed; one male, age 6, kept telling me he was going to marry me. I tried to put him wise: "You can't marry me, you're my cousin", to which he replied, "I'm not, I'm adopted, so I *can* marry you, and I'm *going* to marry you and you can't stop me." Interesting view on matrimony. One male, age 15, said nothing but looked like he wanted to marry me - or at least something along those lines - and wouldn't stop staring at me. There were others but really I can't bring myself to describe them. Oh yes, one little boy kept taking out Mum's Dresden from the display case and saying, "What's this?" and "What's this?" I had to keep taking them off him and trying to impress upon the little lad that they were "extremely valuable Dresden China figures any one of which would cost ten years of your pocket money to replace." I felt like handing him a hairpin and asking him if he would be so kind as to go around and check that all the electrical sockets were working.

After two hours of trying to stop these little monsters from destroying the house I would have quite happily seen them all sent to the workhouse to spend the rest of their lives on the treadmill. But the most extraordinary thing was the complete absence of a single word of correction or instruction or control from the four parents present. Unbelievable! But it got worse, a lot worse.

The first thing I noticed was that the four adults all seemed to be drinking an extraordinary amount and since I was the only bar-person I was run off my feet. I mean it was incredible, I would bring the two brothers a beer each and then go get gin and tonics for the wives, and when I came back with these, the two men would be finished their beers and be looking for more. In the end they just took to going into the fridge and helping themselves. Of course we ran out of beer that way in jig time and they went on to the shorts, drinking everything they could get their hands on. Then they started fighting with their wives, just the odd remark at first but soon, after their tongues had been loosened a bit it was no holds barred and the four of them were at each other hammer and tongs, all of them calling each other the most extraordinary names. And all of this was carried on as if I and Mum simply didn't exist. But what really puzzled me was Mum's attitude. She didn't say a word of reproach to either of her brothers or to any of the children, she just took it all in her stride, as if having her beautiful home turned into a hang-out for low-lifes and delinquents was something she was used to.

The final scene and the final straw was when the two wives were out in the back garden smoking, as Mum politely requested that they not smoke in the house. But instead of sticking to the patio or the paths, the two of them were in the middle of the lawn digging up the grass with their high heels. Then they started shouting at each other. I was inside and could hear every word and it wasn't exactly befitting the season of peace and goodwill, and then suddenly they launched at each other, and these two beauties were tearing each other's hair out, ripping each other's clothes and doing their best to scratch each other's eyes out. They ended up actually rolling around on the grass-now-turned-mud like a couple of heavyweight female mud wrestlers. I've never seen anything like it in my life, but clearly the two husbands had, because one of them just said, "See the girls are at it again." To which the other one replied, "Yeah, looks like it, who's your money on then?"

At that stage Mum had had all she could take and she politely asked her brothers to leave and to take their wives and all their children with them.

By the time we saw the last of them off and checked upstairs to make sure there were no cousins of mine still lurking in a wardrobe somewhere, Mum collapsed into the large sofa, I got her a drink and I just stared at her in disbelief at what I had witnessed.

"So that's my two brothers and their families Judy, what did you think?"

"They seem … eh … quite a bit …eh … different from you, I think, are they? You wouldn't imagine you were so closely related. They don't even look like you, or sound like you."

"That's because we were all born in Huddersfield, but we came down to London when we were children. They seem to have kept the accent more than I have."

"You don't seem to have anything in common with them. I can't believe you even come from the same family."

"You wouldn't believe what it was like growing up in that house with the two of them. I could tell you stories that would make your hair go white, but there's no point, it's all over now. I just wanted you to see them for yourself, so you didn't think it was just me being snobby or something that was the reason why we didn't meet."

"Me think that? Not a chance. Nice wives they have, but maybe we shouldn't invite them both into the house at the same time again."

"I think that might be a good idea."

"You know what Mum - you're all right."

"Why thank you Judy, that's very sweet of you."

"I know all of that was for my benefit by the way. I know why you did it. It all makes sense now."

"What does darling?"

"You, and your brothers. You were right, I did think it was just you being snobby, and that there was probably nothing wrong with your family. I should have trusted you; instead I believed in people I had never even met, over my own mother. I'm sorry Mum, I really am. It must have been very difficult for you, coming from that background, to get to where you are today."

"It was a bit of a struggle all right, but it was worth it." And she gave me the most lovely sad smile.

More than just a bit of a struggle, I thought. And she had done it so that I could have a better life than she had. That made me think of Sally who was going through the same struggle herself, and it made me love the two of them all the more.

"I know sometimes I don't appreciate all the things you do for me, and I'm sorry."

"That's all right love, as long as you've learned a lesson from it. You know what's the most important thing in life?"

"Well I was going to say 'family' but that obviously depends on the family. What then?"

"Loyalty. Mainly to family if they deserve it. Most of them will, some of them won't. You have to decide yourself. Then to your friends, be fiercely loyal to your friends. But whoever it is who deserves your loyalty, to be loyal to *them*, that's the most important thing in life."

"Thanks Mum, I'll try and remember that. But no time for that drink now, we have to go and get Papa. Come on."

"Yes all right, but first I have to turn on the oven and put the turkey in, otherwise there'll be no Christmas dinner will there?" After she had done that I got her keys and ushered her out the front door.

It was lovely seeing Polly, and she had been so happy with her Christmas visitor, that I almost didn't want to separate them. We did invite her to join us but she wouldn't. She said she'd had a lovely few hours and that was enough. They had had lunch together and we needed to get home to our turkey, so we left Polly and drove back across a very quiet London to Barnes.

Christmas dinner was a real treat. We sat at the dining room table for hours, and pulled crackers, and I put a silly paper hat on Dad's head, and Mum served up all the best possible food you could imagine. By the time it came to the cake we had baked together a month before, we were all too full and decided to wait till later. Then we sat down together in the family room which we hadn't done for a long time, and me and Mum watched TV while Papa stared into the fire.

When we were going up to bed that night I said to Mum, "Well that's Christmas over and we survived. Tell you what though - that was a good idea of yours leaving Papa over to Polly."

"Yes Judy, there are some things I will never subject your poor father to, and my brothers and their wives are one of them. Good night darling."

"Good night Mummy, and thank you for everything." As I said we have our ups and downs me and Mum, well this Christmas was definitely one of the ups.

****

Very early in the New Year my father and Polly got into their extra-long Mercedes again and rolled down the drive and out the gate on the first few feet of a journey that would take them thousands of miles all over Europe. Mum and I had given them a good send-off a couple of nights before, on New Year's Eve, when we all went to a posh restaurant and had a fantastic meal. One nice thing happened at the restaurant which meant a lot to all of us. About half-way through our meal we noticed a large party at a near-by table looking at us and mentioning Dad's name. Then one of them came over, very politely and apologetically, and said:

"Excuse me, I'm really sorry for interrupting your meal, but you see, some of us were at Mr Jones's concert in Cardiff, and I just wanted to say it was a pleasure to hear you play, sir," (and here he addressed Papa directly which was really nice, instead of just talking *about* him if you know what I mean) "and there wasn't a single member of the audience who wasn't delighted they came that night to hear you play. So I just wanted to say thank you. Enjoy your meal. Bye."

And as he went back to his table Polly had to take out a hankie and dab her eyes while Papa sat there with a little smile on his face. Wonderful.

But after Papa and Polly had left, me and Mum were so lonely and found the house so quiet and empty. We went back inside and we were just about to go into the family room when Mum stopped.

"No, I'm not going in there," she said. "Not without him, not till he gets back." And I thought, "Wow, someone's changed a lot." You see, I'd known they weren't really in love at all, and hadn't been for some time, not in my time anyway and maybe not even before that. But now that Mum had lost Papa, mentally at least, and she maybe was afraid of losing him completely to Polly, it looked like she was beginning to fall in love with him all over again. And not an Amortentia Love Potion in sight!

****

We kept track of their progress by means of the postcards Polly regularly sent from every city they visited. Every one of them went into the scrapbooks, and I have them all here, the whole list of cities Polly read out to Papa. I also have the reviews from every European paper, totally incomprehensible for the most part as they are in Spanish, Portuguese, Italian, German, etc, etc. but where I could get a translation on the internet I've put those in too. Polly was doing a great job as usual but we decided to go out and join them at half-term, by which time they would be in Munich.

Meanwhile I had to go back to school and my friends which was really great. The first day back was a half-day and consisted merely of seeing where we were in each subject and catching up on the gossip. The big talking point was of course Natalie Gorman and whether she was going to be expelled or not. She did look a bit chastened all right and didn't even retaliate against a few of the remarks along the lines of: "Look who's still here, didn't expect to see you again Natalie." But by the end of the week when she was still there, she was back to her usual cocky, obnoxious self. And she made it known to everyone that her father had used some of his "sevens" to fund the building of a new gymnasium to be known as the Natalie Gorman Hall. I know, it would make you sick, but at least the school was getting something out if it I suppose.

****

By February I was getting really excited about the prospect of seeing Papa in Munich at the middle of the month, and when the time came and once again we were sitting at the back of the plane with an empty seat between us (Mum still hadn't mastered the art of leaving the house in time so we're not last to check in) I couldn't sit still with the excitement. I kept talking at full speed, saying to Mum, "Isn't this great? Remember the last time we did this? Last July only. And how upset I was. You kept telling me you'd kill me if I didn't stop crying. And the stewardess got all upset too, and got me loads of tissues, but I still couldn't stop crying. We didn't know if Papa was alive or dead, remember? And we'd no idea what we'd find when we got to the hospital. And now look at us, flying to Munich again, but this time to see him play the piano in a big concert hall. It's unbelievable. Sorry I know I'm sounding like Polly now so I'll stop …" And I stopped … "But isn't it great?"

It was just like arriving at the lovely hotel in Cardiff all over again, getting into our Munich hotel, and meeting Polly and Papa in Papa's room. I haven't stayed in a lot of international five star hotels but from what I've seen they do appear to be all pretty samey. Sorry - but they do. Then the dinner, and the concert hall the following night, all wonderful of course, but just a bit samey, even though the concert hall was nothing less than the Altes Residenz, a concert hall so old that Mozart himself had conducted the premieres of some of his operas there.

There was one incredible surprise, however, in store for us. After the concert, which went perfectly according to our usual routine, we all met back in the dressing room where a note was handed in addressed to Mr Jones. It was a letter from - guess who - Prof Meyerhofer, who had heard Papa was playing there, and had come up from the hospital near Salzburg specially to see him. Thank God I didn't see the little Professor and neither did Papa, until after the performance. If I had seen him I would have been a basket case throughout the recital worrying that Papa might spot him too, and if Papa had seen him I had no idea how he would have taken it. He might have thought the men in white coats had come to take him away again.

So we sent the Stage Doorman who had delivered the letter back out to find the Professor and a minute later a timid knock on the dressing room door announced his arrival. In he came, looking smaller even than I remembered, and with his big head and huge eyes he looked more Gollum-like than ever. All that was missing was the white coat. Of course he hadn't expected me and

142

Mum to be there too, and when he saw us he was overwhelmed.

"My dear Mrs Yones, and my dear Miss Yones who has grown so tall since I am seeing her last time, how wonderful to see you both again. And this lovely lady who looks after my patient so well, excuse me ...?"

"This is Polly, our nurse," introduced Mum. "Polly, this is Professor Meyerhofer." At the mention of his name we all - even the professor himself - automatically looked over to where my father was sitting at his dressing table, but happily there was no reaction. This must have emboldened the little old psychiatrist to take a closer look at his star patient, and as he went cautiously towards him we all held our breath.

"Mr Yones, I wish to congratulate you on your playing, and thank you for a most enjoyable evening of beautiful music." There was no reaction at all from Papa so the professor just took another really close look at him and left it at that.

"My dears, it is so wonderful to see you all again, and what an incredible way this case has turned out. I wish I could take some credit for it but absolutely no it is nothing to do with me or the treatment we gave Mr Yones in the hospital. Such cases do occur of course, but they are very rare and we have no way of predicting them. I am a scientist and I do not believe in miracles, but this... this is remarkable. All I can say is that you have all done a remarkably good job in helping Mr Yones make this achievement."

I was too chuffed to say anything, remembering my own and Polly's use of the "M" word the first time Papa had played, and we looked at each other and smiled. But Mum was remembering something else - her manners. "Please Professor Meyerhofer," she said. "Won't you come back to our hotel with us and have something to eat or a drink?"

"Dear lady I would love to but sadly I cannot stay long as I have to take a train back home very soon. I just wanted to see my patient and what a wonderful surprise to see you both too and to meet your excellent nurse Polly. I am so pleased. But now forgive me but I must be leaving. But I am almost forgetting. I am now on the computer technology called the email and here is my address. Please Miss Yones to keep in touch and let me know everything that is happening to your father. I will be so interested to hear all. " I took the card and promised I would keep in touch, and with that he shook hands with all of us and backed out of the dressing room as if we were royalty, leaving us all in a daze.

"Well," Polly was the first to speak. "Isn't he a nice little fellow." No-one could have put it any better than that.

****

After the Munich concert Mum and I went home and A few days later I went back to school. Papa and Polly continued with their European Tour, playing to packed concert halls and enthusiastic reviews everywhere they went.

School continued on as usual heading into the Easter holidays and there was nothing to break up its tedious monotony. I couldn't wait for Dad to be finished his tour and come back home to us.

At the end of May they finally played their final concert in the Salle Pleyel in Paris and the following afternoon they boarded the Eurostar, car, driver and all, and six hours later they were turning in our gates and we were running out to greet them.

I must admit I was expecting Dad to have improved more after his recent attempts at smiling and ever so slight interaction with us, and so I was really disappointed when I saw him. I had never seen him looking so tired, not since we got him home the first time from Austria. I hadn't seen him in over two months and he had visibly aged too. Of course I didn't let on and did everything I could to make the homecoming a great celebration but underneath I was worried. Polly stayed the night at our insistence and the following day I managed to get her alone for a moment.

"Polly," I started carefully.

"Yes love, I know what you're going to say. I knew nothing would get past you."

"What?"

"You think he's looking tired, don't you?"

"Then it must be true. I'm right aren't I?"

"Yes, I'm afraid so, you're right. He is exhausted and he needs a really long rest. We didn't have any problems, he played every night and gave a full recital, not like in Cardiff, but I could see it becoming a greater and greater effort for him every night. I'm just so glad we're home and I pray he doesn't have to do another concert for at least six months."

Unfortunately Polly hadn't reckoned with a certain ambitious agent fond of wearing her sunglasses on her head. Of course Ms Bleating was soon buzzing up our drive in her little cabriolet, annoying the neighbours no doubt with the loud music from her car radio. And there she was again, sunglasses on barnet, little two-piece suit, and a list of 40 concert engagements in the United States of America starting with Carnegie Hall in New York in July! I didn't know whether to laugh or cry but Mummy was ecstatic. New York - her favourite city in the world - even though she'd only been there once. And of course this Bleating bint kept calling it the "Big Apple", a phrase I have heard before and which never ceases to irritate me. At this stage I was beginning to wonder if my initial dislike of the woman had been that far out after all.

"Just imagine," she was drawling in that irritating mid-Atlantic twang she has, "The Big Apple in July, and if we're lucky we can get him onto Jay Leno - I've got really good contacts there!" Then she started listing off a seemingly endless number of US cities most of which, even if I had heard the name, meant nothing to me, and while I was listening to this catalogue of engagements which I was becoming more and more convinced Papa would not be up to, and while the agent kept repeating, "Then on the 21st he plays here, after that on the 29th he plays here ..." it suddenly dawned on me what was wrong with this woman and why I had disliked her so much from the start - and it wasn't anything to do with the sunglasses on her head, or

146

the noisy little sports car or the mid-Atlantic drawl. No, it was something far deeper and more revealing than any of these irritating characteristics. It was the fact that she never referred to Papa by anything other than "he" or "him", she never used his name, which showed that for her he simply wasn't a person. That was utterly revealing of the character of the woman and utterly unforgivable. And as she went on and on with this interminable list of concerts something else suddenly dawned on me too, and I couldn't believe how long it had taken me to realise this simple fact: she wasn't doing any of this for Papa, or even for us, she was doing it all for Samantha Bleating. Then I remembered the contract I had seen briefly six months ago in which I had noticed that this agent was taking a whopping 30% of everything Dad earned. I felt such a fool for not realising it earlier, but when I looked at Mum lapping up every word from this dreadful woman I could see she hadn't a clue what was going on. This woman saw Dad as her own personal goose laying the golden eggs, and she was obviously determined to get her hands on as many of them as possible - even if the goose died in the process. Somebody had to put a stop to it now and it had to be me.

"Thank you Ms Bleating for all of that," I said, trying not to make it too obvious, "Can we have a think about it and we will get back to you."

"Of course, but which aspect of the tour do you need to think about exactly?"

"Well every aspect actually, the whole tour in fact. You see, my father is very tired after the hectic schedule of the last tour of Europe - you probably wouldn't have noticed - and I really think he needs a rest before embarking upon any other prolonged series of engagements." I listened to myself and couldn't believe what I was coming out with, it sounded so good. Mother couldn't believe what I was coming out with either, but not for the same reason.

"Judy really," she said, "Your father is fine. Now let Ms Bleating continue with her list of engagements. "Please excuse my daughter's rudeness, Ms Bleating, do go on."

"Mother. I really think we need to discuss this before we make any commitment."

"I don't think your daughter understands," the agent went on in her smarmy tone. "All of these dates in America are finalised, all contracts have been signed."

"Signed?" my mother was puzzled, "We didn't sign anything relating to these engagements."

"No of course not," and here she gave this sickening guffaw. "You don't need to sign anything, that's why I'm here. I signed them all on your behalf, in accordance with the contract we have."

"Oh yes, of course," my mother replied lamely.

"Let me get this straight," I took over, "My mother signed a contract allowing you to decide where and when and how often my father plays in public for the next three years? With no limit over the number of concerts he is expected to play? Is that what you're saying?"

"Shouldn't we leave this discussion up to the adults here, don't you think Mrs Jones? Those of us capable of understanding it." That was a big mistake.

"Actually I think you should answer my daughter's question, as I was not aware that our contract gave you such complete control over my husband's career, especially as regards how often he must play."

"In that case I suggest you read the contract more closely Mrs Jones, as that is exactly what it does. He plays whenever and wherever and however often I get him engagements to play, whether you like it or not. And now if you will excuse me I am very busy." With that she stormed out of the room and I followed her out just in time to see her actually push past my poor father in the hall, as she made her exit. I suppose he must have heard the raised voices and come out of the family room just then, as he had this really sad puzzled look on his face. The last we heard of her was the wheels of her vile sports car churning up the gravel on our drive. I brought Dad back into the family room and sat him down in his chair, then went back into Mum.

"Mum, what have you done? How could you sign such a contract?" I asked her, though she looked so shocked I couldn't be too hard on her.

"I don't know ... I didn't realise ... I never thought she could come up with so many ... Yes I know, I gave her complete control over organising your father's concerts, because she was a professional and she knew about it. I just never thought there could possibly be so many in such a short period of time. I just never imagined..."

"Oh God Mum, he can't do all of these concerts in America. He's exhausted already. This tour will kill him."

Chapter Seven - Papa Becomes a World-Famous Pianist and Plays in Carnegie Hall but When a Riot Ensues He Gives it All Up

The first thing Mum did was to get her lawyer to check the contract and give us his opinion. Then we needed to consult Polly and see exactly what she thought. So the next day, after Mum had talked to her lawyer and he was getting stuck in, the three of us sat around the dining table and Mum, looking more humble than I have ever seen her, made a full and contrite confession.

"Polly," she started off hesitantly, "I've done something dreadful and we're in a bit of a mess." Then she explained about the contract and the Bleating woman and her list of US engagements and asked her did she think Papa would be able for any of it.

"How many concerts altogether?" Polly asked.

"Forty," I answered as Mum was too ashamed to admit it.

"Forty? What kind of a woman is this? Does she not realise Jack's condition? She must be totally inhuman. There's no way Jack can face anything like that number of concerts, not after the last four months in Europe. It's just impossible. What happens if we refuse?"

"That's for the lawyer to advise. She'll probably sue us for breach of contract."

"All I can say is, if we make him do all these concerts in America it will be the death of him." And she burst into tears, poor Polly.

A week later (you know the way lawyers like to take their time) we had our official legal advice, in the form of a letter which Mummy interpreted for us as Polly and I once again sat at the dining room table.

"Right, there's some good news here but not much. Basically what the lawyer is saying is we don't have a leg to stand on. If we refuse to do any of the dates, we will be sued for breach of contract and we will probably lose the case. But he suggests that we at least start the tour, which shows good faith, play the New York concert anyway, and then after that, if we don't think Jack is up to continuing, we can pull out claiming ill-health and even if she sues us then, a Judge would be more inclined to come down on our side considering Jack's state of mind. So - what do you think?"

"I suppose we have no choice," said Polly, "He should be all right for one concert there anyway. It's now the end of May, that gives Jack two months to rest."

"Looks like we're going to the 'Big Apple' - Hooray!" I added sarcastically.

****

We obviously didn't say anything to Papa about a possible tour of the United States, just doing what we could to prepare him for another flight and a trip to New York.

"This will be a really big plane Papa," I knelt down beside him showing him some pictures I'd got off the internet of a wide-bodied aircraft. "It's called a Jumbo Jet." I know no one calls them Jumbo Jets any more - way naff - but I thought he might like the name, considering, you know.

"See all the rows of seats, and two aisles, plenty of room to walk around, because it's a long flight, six or seven hours." No interest. "And you'll be able to watch movies," No interest. "And you'll get two meals, so twice as much to eat." Big smile. I think my Dad's the only person I know who really loves airplane food.

While all the preparations were being made for New York I had to finish up in school, which involved one term of tennis which Sally and I were both hopeless at, and guess who was the captain of the tennis team? Yup, the beautiful, the brainy, and now the athletic Miss Natalie Gorman! The game of tennis was made for someone like Natalie as it gave her endless opportunities to practise what she called "gamesmanship" - cheating to you and me. Firing the ball directly at her opponent's body; lobbing it high into the air if the sun was in her opponent's eyes; spending ages tying her shoe laces to make her opponent nervous on a break point and other time wasting; pretending not to be ready when her opponent is about to serve; changing racquets mid-game, and of course challenging every single ball that was on the line in such a

152

way that the umpire was subtly influenced or even intimidated into a more favourable attitude towards her. All these tactics or strategies she had been well coached in by her parents, who used to sit by the court side in their own tennis gear (why I have no idea, and they looked really strange in it as they were a good bit older than you would have expected) and cheer on their darling daughter in a way that added its own intimidation to whatever poor girl she was up against. They even made noises when the other girl was serving, deliberately trying to put her off. Unbelievable! Sally and I were far better off out of it.

End of year exams came and went without any further controversy, and even Sally's father went back to being his usual grumpy slobby self (her words not mine) so she gave up the idea that he was having an affair. In early July we got our holidays and we had exactly a week to get ready for the big trip.

The Bleating woman hadn't been to the house since the last dreadful time, but she had sent a number of emails to Mum about arrangements and she was going to turn up in New York if we were really out of luck. We were flying on a Friday with his concert on the Sunday so we had a day in between to recover. The only problem was that Papa couldn't bring his own piano, it being too far and too expensive to transport across the Atlantic. I wasn't surprised, and hoped he would be OK without it. She did at least let us have the big car again to take us to the airport; otherwise with all the bags we would have needed two taxis. So the four of us sat in the huge long Mercedes and I must say, all things considered, Papa seemed happy enough, and Mum and Polly, though nervous, were in pretty good form.

We got through Check-in and Security this time without any fuss, and even though I had been dreading it, we got Papa onto the plane first time without a hitch. I just kept promising him chocolate bars and he just kept going. On the plane we were somewhere around the middle on the left-hand side with two pairs of window and aisle seats. Papa and I sat in one pair where we were able to hold hands on take-off, while Mum and Polly were behind us. For most of the flight Papa just stared out the window as if he couldn't get enough of looking at sky and clouds. Except of course when the meals arrived, and because it was such a long flight there were two of them - three actually if you count one of Mum's which she couldn't face and passed on to us. He did however acquire one new trick, which although it was embarrassing, showed perhaps that he might be recovering in some strange way.

Soon after take-off Papa started pressing the light buttons over our heads, on and off, on and off. It was harmless enough and seemed to amuse him. But then he hit the call button, and when a stewardess arrived pronto I had to apologise and say we didn't really need anything. The smiling stewardess just reached over and turned off the light. Papa however was rather smitten by this beautiful apparition, and when a minute later he hit the call button again, and again the same beautiful smiling face appeared, he was hooked.

"Sorry, it was a mistake. False alarm. My father hit the button by mistake," I had to explain, and the stewardess smiled politely again and turned off the light. And then Papa gave her a big smile which I thought was great, but Mum didn't see it like that. The next hour of the flight consisted in a battle between me and Papa to stop him summoning up the lovely stewardess every five minutes by means of the magic button, and giving her a big smile any time she turned up. Polly sitting behind us, remarked after a while, "I think Jack's got the hang of that call button all right."

"He seems to have got the hang of that smile too. If he doesn't stop I'm going to have to sit somewhere else," said Mum. But that wasn't necessary as the stewardess herself gave up coming when she got the picture, and the light stayed on for the rest of the trip.

When we touched down in New York it was still mid afternoon - they do this funny thing with the time over there that I must tell you about. Don't know why, but they don't like to have the same time as us - bit like their English spelling I suppose - and so they're five hours behind. So when you get there instead of it being time for bed, it's not even tea time, and you've still got an extra five hours of daylight to get through. Very strange. Still Papa didn't mind as it gave him an extra meal. But first we had to get to the hotel.

Nothing could have prepared us for New York City in July. Getting out of the Arrivals Terminal and into a taxi was all right, though it was a bit of a squeeze with four of us in one taxi and our five suitcases sticking out of the boot (they don't make the cars there as big as they used to which is a pity, not to mention the fact that our taxi driver looked nothing like Robert de Niro) but when we got into Manhattan and got stuck in traffic we really began to swelter. There was no air conditioning in the cab and opening a window just made it hotter. Nevertheless, I enjoyed looking at the amazing skyscrapers which seemed to go on up for ever. I know I probably should be more cool about them but WOW! I'd never seen anything like it in my life. If you took the NatWest Tower or what is it Canary Wharf and doubled it you'd get an idea of how tall these building are. But even then you'd need to have about a hundred of them all side by side in one small area to get a feel for New York City. And then there's the heat and the noise, both of which hit you like a smack in the face. And the crowds - another smack in the face. As we neared the hotel we passed Carnegie Hall - at least Bleating had put us in a hotel nearby. I was the first to spot it and started shouting,

"Look there's Carnegie Hall, that's where we're going to be!" And the taxi driver said, "You folks going to a show?"

"Eh, yes, my father is playing the piano there on Sunday night," I explained cautiously.

"Playin de piana, ya don't say! I usta play de piana but I never practised enough. My Ma usta say to me, if ya don't practise you won't get to Carnegie Hall. But what did I care, I was only a kid. Now I drive a cab and I get to Carnegie Hall all de time. What's de difference?"

"Yes that's a very good point," I replied, "Oh look, there's our hotel. Just stop here please." The driver stopped right outside and since he had to haul all our suitcases out of the boot I gave him a big tip. Everybody has to be tipped here in NYC, you'd need to have a sackful of change with you to hand out enough tips everywhere you go. You feel like Good King Wenceslas on the Feast of Stephen. The Hotel porters came out to the taxi when they saw us and brought in all the cases (more tips). Then the doorman held the door open for us (big tip otherwise next time you have to open the door yourself) and we proceeded grandly up to the Reception Desk. Having checked in, a different pair of boys called Bell-Hops helped us upstairs with our bags (more tips) and we were finally installed in our two-bedroom suite way up on the 35th floor. The rooms were enormous and the view! - the view was pretty much into another tall building about ten yards away.

Anybody who travels a lot likes to talk about this thing they call jet-lag, which proves that they travel a lot. Well I've got it sussed. if you arrive somewhere and you have to put your watch back a few hours, you just go have a lie down for that number of hours and then pretend they weren't there. If it happens the other way and you're a few hours ahead you just stay up later. What's the big deal? So since we had five hours extra time everybody tried out my theory and we all had a long nap and then a nice shower or bath to use up the extra time we didn't want, and then went down to the dining room for dinner at the normal time. Papa seemed to be enjoying himself and didn't appear to be too tired from the journey so we were beginning to worry a bit less about the long concert schedule. Anyway we would cross that bridge when we came to it, and first we had to get through the Carnegie Hall recital.

The next day started off bad - real bad. We'd had a nice dinner and gone to bed about 11.00 New York time, but we couldn't wake up Papa the next morning. Breakfast was served until 10.00 and even getting it brought up to the room and waving the bacon and eggs under his nose like a dose of smelling salts didn't do the trick. He just wouldn't wake up. By 12.00 the Bleating woman was ringing up and telling us that we were so lucky and she'd worked really hard and got Dad onto this late night show with this guy called Jay Leno but he didn't have to stay up late, just do the recording in the afternoon, like the ones he did at home. So we had to be in the studio beside somewhere called Radio City to record Dad's piece at three. Mum said, "That's impossible we're in the middle of New York and couldn't possibly get to another city by three o'clock." Then she found out Radio City was a TV studio in the Rockefeller Center about five blocks away. By one o'clock Dad finally began to stir and we left him alone to have a shower and get dressed but even after that he still appeared a bit groggy. Then we had to get him lunch downstairs and rush him out into the street to get a taxi.

"At least it's Saturday afternoon so the traffic shouldn't be too bad, " I said as we got in. Pretty soon I found out that there's two types of traffic in New York: when it's light you could walk faster, and when it's heavy you could walk twice as fast. So it took us about half an hour to get to the place but we were there by three, and they seemed to be expecting us all right because as soon as we mentioned Dad's name we were ushered in and given the VIP treatment, with a couple of assistants bringing

Polly and Dad off in one direction to the studio to rehearse and record his performance, while Mum and I were ushered off to what they call the Green Room - couldn't understand why as there wasn't a spot of green in it. Plenty of beige though. But it was very nice, like the VIP Lounge in the airport all over again with free drinks and tea and coffee and tons of food. Just as well as we had to wait there about two hours. The great thing was, though, there were TVs all around the walls, some of them blank and some of them showing the insides of studios or TV programs. Then after about an hour we couldn't believe our eyes but Dad appeared on one of the TVs sitting at a piano with Polly beside him, appearing to be playing although we couldn't hear any sound. He stopped and started a few times, as instructed by Polly, and then seemed to play for about five minutes without a break. It seemed to go fine as from what we could see, Polly looked perfectly happy and a sort of stage manager guy I suppose came over to them and applauded Dad and showed them off the stage. After that we just had to wait for them to turn up in the Green Room which they duly did, accompanied by the guy we'd seen on the TV.

"Hi I'm Donnie," says this guy as they come in. Donnie was flamboyantly dressed with a scarf around his shoulders and hair that looked like it had been blow-dried about two minutes ago. "That was super. The recording went perfectly and Mr Jones played beautifully." At this point Mr Jones had spotted all the food and was making a bee line for the buffet tables. Unfazed, our friend Donnie continued, "Mr Leno sends his apologies that he couldn't be here to meet you personally, but he has been delayed getting into the city. I hope you'll watch the show tonight and you'll see Mr Jones's performance." He obviously had been thinking of showing us out at that point but when he saw Dad scoffing as much food as he could get his hands on, he reconsidered.

"Maybe I'll just let you relax here for a little while and come back to you a bit later."

"That would be very kind of you, Donnie," said Mum giving Dad an embarrassed look, "I'm sure we'll be ready to leave quite soon."

"Oh no hurry," said Donnie, "Take all the time you like." And then he added in a whisper, "It's actually great to see someone enjoying the food here. Most of the stars we get in are too -" (and here he stroked the tip of his nose with a forefinger) "- to eat, if you know what I mean."

Ten minutes later the door was flung open and I was astounded to see the famous Jay Leno striding into the room, preceded by the famous Jay Leno chin.

"I got here quicker than I expected," he was saying "So I just had to come and meet you!" We bounced up out of our chairs and met him halfway across the room where we shook hands and introduced ourselves.

"And this must be your famous father," Jay added, walking over towards Dad who was behind the buffet table still scoffing away. But he must have got a fright when he saw this larger-than-life figure heading for him with his hand outstretched - or maybe he thought the big guy was after his grub - because Dad immediately picked up as many buns and profiteroles as he could and started pelting the great Jay Leno with them.

"Jack!" cried Mum and Polly together.

"Dad!" cried myself joining in. But all to no avail. Dad was in fighting form and all poor Mr Leno could do was pretty much stand there and take a pasting. I ran into the line of fire and disarmed the offender but not before considerable damage was done to:

A. Jay Leno's appearance

B. Dad's chances of making it as a chat-show guest

C. Our reputation

But Jay, showing the good humour and tolerance for which he was famed, shook it all off with a joke:

"It was only a matter of time before my show turned into a cream cake fight."

At that point we all beat a retreat and Mum and Polly, after trying to wipe some of the goo off our host, were politely shown out, along with myself and a not-at-all-contrite-looking Dad still with an éclair in his fist. The ladies decided they would like to walk back to the hotel and look at some of the shops along the way, as they hadn't seen any of the city yet. I had to get Dad back in a taxi of course as it was too far to walk. So Mum and Polly went off down the street while I looked around for an empty cab. Only problem was, there weren't any. I mean there were lots of cabs but they were all full. The streets were really crowded and I could feel Papa tensing up. He didn't like crowds at all and as he started making little squeaky noises I knew I had to get him back to the hotel as soon as possible.

I don't know if you know New York, but if you want to get a taxi you practically have to stand out in the middle of the street to try and hail one down. So I had the choice of either leaving Papa alone on the footpath with the crowds of people or taking him out into the traffic with me. Cursing myself for not having thought of this before I let Mum and Polly go, I tried to do a bit of both. The result was that between the people and the cars, Papa was in an awful state when we finally managed to find an empty cab. Giving the driver the name of the hotel the two of us got into the back, Papa doing his monkey noises a bit. I thought we were safe then but of all the taxi drivers in NYC we had to get into a cab with one who was a complete psychopath. First he was driving like a lunatic, speeding where there was a gap in the traffic, and then having to stand on the brakes, so the two of us were being thrown around the back seat like it was a fairground ride. Then the cursing and blowing his horn at every other driver. Of course Papa was getting really scared and the monkey noises got a bit worse. So after a few minutes this creature behind the wheel starts on us: "Hey what's with this guy? Some kind of a nut? What's with de chimp impersonation? You wanna go to de Zoo? I can take ya to de Zoo, it's in Central Park." That was enough.

"Stop!" I yelled. "Stop the car, we're getting out. Here, right here."

"What? What did I say?" He found a gap in the traffic and screeched over to the curb. I got Papa out of the back seat and threw in a ten dollar bill.

"There's only one animal in this cab and it's not my father," I said and slammed the door.

We were both so upset at this stage we just stood on the side of the street and I hugged Dad really tight. And the amazing thing was, he put his arms around my shoulders and hugged me back! That had never happened before, it was the first time he had ever responded like that, and I just burst into tears in a mixture of frustration and rage and relief and joy. And we stood there for ages in the middle of Sixth Avenue hugging each other. Then I looked at my map and up at the street signs and I realised we were only one block away from the hotel - we were on the right street, we just had to get from Sixth to Seventh Avenues - so slowly and steadily we made our way along the street until we finally got back to our hotel.

"It's OK Papa, we're back now safe and sound." I said to him as I settled him into a chair. "We're not going anywhere again until tomorrow. And we won't tell anyone about what happened, we'll just forget about it, OK?"

Pretty soon Mum and Polly came in the door. At least I thought it was them but couldn't see anything at first except a number of huge shopping bags. They'd managed to find a couple of shops still open, and had made a few select purchases each. After they had showed me and Papa all their buys it was time for dinner and they decided to go downstairs to the dining room with Dad. I had other ideas.

"Right, you go downstairs," I said, "But there's a 40 inch TV in my room, and air conditioning and a big bath, and I believe there's something called room service that they do quite well here, so I for one am not moving out of that bedroom for the next twenty-four hours at least. Anyone who wants me you know where I'll be. But make sure you're back up in time to see Papa on the Tonight Show." They promised they would and went downstairs to the dining room.

I had the most relaxing few hours ever, and when the time came for Leno the four of us sat around watching the show till they had Papa on doing his piece. And Jay Leno said something rather extraordinary in his introduction. He said he had had the pleasure of meeting Mr Jones himself and that all his colleagues on the show agreed with him, that he was not just a musical genius but a real gentleman. I couldn't believe my ears.

****

The following day at about five we all left the hotel together to walk the short distance to the concert hall so Papa could have a look at the piano and get changed and relax in his dressing room before his concert started at 8.00. I'll never forget arriving at that famous venue, possibly the most famous concert hall in the world, especially for pianists, New York's Carnegie Hall. It's the Mecca for all aspiring classical musicians, the one venue in the world that everyone wants to play in, and here we were going in the grand entrance and announcing ourselves, and my own father was going to play in that hallowed musical sanctuary. I couldn't believe it, I really couldn't. Papa seemed all right up until then, and gave no hint of the disaster that lay ahead.

Just finding your way around Carnegie Hall is a challenge in itself, I mean it's vast, it feels like the inside of Wembley Stadium. Getting from the dressing room to the stage, when you walk at Papa's pace took about ten minutes. Polly was with him in the dressing room of course, and would go on stage with him. Mum was in the audience and I was going to stay in the wings even though thankfully we had got Dad off the bell-ringing routine by the end of the UK concert tour. I just liked to be there for him. So it got to about a quarter to eight and Papa and Polly and I were sitting quietly in the dressing room, obviously in a dreadful state of nerves but trying not to show it. Papa was the only one who didn't seem nervous, but then I never knew what was going on inside his head. And just then the door flew open and that awful Bleating woman was standing there, saying she'd just flown in specially to be here, and wishing us luck and saying she'd be in the audience and fingers crossed and all this rubbish which we absolutely did not need at that particular moment. The worst thing was, it was obvious she had been drinking - probably on the plane, bad idea. She was louder than usual and had that look about her that reminded me of lunching ladies. I got her out as quickly as I could but I could see how it affected Papa. He hadn't forgotten the last occasion they met at home and even the sound of her voice I could see had a terribly negative effect on him.

I wanted to give out about her to Polly of course, but I knew that would only make things worse. We had to remain cool and serene and try to get Papa to the edge of the stage as quietly and as calmly as possible. Another knock on the door but it was the stage manager this time, giving us the ten minutes' notice we had requested. So we got Papa to his feet, and together the three of us made the long slow walk to the edge of the stage. If you've never seen the stage of Carnegie Hall you couldn't imagine it - it is enormous, about the size of a football pitch. And completely bare except for the piano, which, even though it was an eight-foot long concert grand, looked tiny in the middle of that vast empty space. For any concert pianist that must be the most terrifying walk in their entire career, from the wings to the piano on the stage of Carnegie Hall.

Eight o'clock came and everyone was in their seats, the lights went down and the stage manager behind us whispered that they could go, and Polly and my father started their long scary walk together as the audience burst into applause. They both sat down and the audience fell silent. Papa put his hands up on the keyboard and there was a moment's silence while everyone held their breath, and then it started, the opening bars of "Les jeux d'eau a la Villa d'Este" - or what I called the Italian Villa water fountains piece. And even though I have now heard that piece of music I'd say a hundred times, it still has this amazing effect on me. And on every member of the audience too I'd say as when he finished there was a moment of silence and then an absolute torrent of cheering and applause like nothing I had ever heard in any of the concerts I had been to. This was probably because of the sheer size of the hall and the number of people in the audience - 2,804 to be precise. Polly and Papa stood up and made a little bow and as they sat down again the audience immediately cut out the applause, as if someone had turned off a switch. And then we heard it - everyone in the hall must have heard it - just as the audience hit the off button, that hideous drawl from the drunken Bleating woman:

"Oh yah, he is a client of mine, I'm very pleased with him." Someone else in the audience then said "Hush" but it was too late.

I immediately looked over at Papa and could see his shoulders tighten and his head give a kind of jerk which I was terrified to see because I knew exactly what it meant. I've seen it so many times in horses, the head just pulls up a bit and the ears go back. It's a very primitive animal reaction and it can only mean one thing: Refusal. In a horse coming up to a fence it means you'll probably end up over the horse's neck. In a concert pianist sitting at a piano in the middle of the stage of Carnegie Hall it spells disaster. I waited at the edge of the stage praying in silence; the audience sat patiently and quietly in their seats. I could barely hear Polly's whispered words of encouragement which, if given a chance, probably would have worked. But then unbelievably it happened again - that woman's voice again:

"Oh come on Jack, do be a darling and play something nice for us." That was too much for some of the less self-controlled members of the audience and they burst out laughing. Papa's recital was doomed. Whether he thought the laughing was aimed at him, or whether it was just the sound of the agent's voice, I don't know but he immediately started up with the monkey noises, banged the lid down on the keys and stood up. The next two minutes will forever be the worst two minutes of my life. Papa shrugged off Polly's hand and strode to the front of the stage where he proceeded to march up and down staring at the audience with the utmost hostility while he went on chittering and squeaking and waving his arms. The audience's reaction was in places let us say unrestrained. Both Polly and myself ran for him but with the size of the stage by the time we got to him he'd done enough damage to ensure his debut performance in the world's most famous concert hall would also be his last. We managed at least to get him to come with us, and eventually got him off the stage, Polly and myself in tears and Papa not much better. By now the audience was in uproar, as those few who had laughed at Papa and, I must admit, booed him when he was at his worst, were now being attacked by the better mannered members who were shouting "Shame on you" or words to that effect, defending Papa and telling them they were a disgrace. It very nearly descended into a saloon brawl like you'd see in a Western movie.

We finally got Papa back to his dressing room and Mum arrived. We locked the door and just sat there stunned and in tears, unable to believe it had all become such a complete disaster so quickly. There was uproar outside our door too, but we refused to open it and waited until everyone had given up and gone away. We got Papa back into his ordinary clothes and an hour later I unlocked the door and we made our way back to our hotel. The following day we checked out of our hotel, took a taxi to the airport and got the first available flight home to London. Passing through JFK Airport it was impossible not to notice the headlines in some of the more popular press about "Riots in Carnegie Hall". I didn't want to look and I tried not to but the last headline I saw as I passed the last newsagent before boarding the plane sort of stuck in my mind. It said, "You Can't Make Monkeys out of Us."

****

Chapter Eight - Papa Starts Trading Forex and Gets a Job Working for the Government

They do say there's no place like home and there are times when I must agree; getting back home from New York was definitely one of them. For the rest of that summer I just kept saying to myself and to anyone else who would listen, "No-one died. We're all still alive, we have a lovely home, the three of us are together, and Papa's getting better. Forget New York." Easier said than done, however, when the news came that Bleating was being sued by the promoter who booked Papa for Carnegie Hall, and she in turn was suing us. Nice one, when you consider the whole disaster had been pretty much her fault. Mum just told me the facts and said there was nothing to worry about, that her lawyer would handle it, so I tried not to think about it and got on with the rest of the holidays.

One thing that became clear over the course of the next few weeks was that Papa was probably finished with the piano. Not just from a professional point of view as a concert pianist; that was definitely over, all of us were agreed on that, but also as any kind of pianist. I felt it would be a pity if he didn't play again at home, but from the time we arrived back from New York he never went near the piano. No amount of encouragement from myself or Polly could get him to play and, ever mindful of

Professor Meyerhofer's advice, I didn't want to push him too much. In the end Polly and I agreed, just like after the very first occasion, that "He'll play again when he wants to." But that soon turned into, "He'll play again if he wants to" and soon after that we stopped saying it completely.

I got in touch with Sally as soon as I felt up to seeing any of my friends and caught up on her summer so far. But even she didn't have anything amusing to cheer me up with, no news at all really. We went to a movie together, and I met one or two of the others, and pretty soon it was time to go back to school. The first person I met when I walked in the school gates was Sally, which was nice. The second person I met was Natalie Gorman which wasn't.

"I hear your father made a bit of a fool of himself in New York," was her friendly opening greeting, while all her hench-women stood around smirking.

"Ignore her," said Sally beside me as we tried to get past and into school.

"Or should I say, 'made a bit of a monkey of himself'."

I stopped and stared at her.

"Don't bother Judy," said Sally, "She's not worth it."

"Natalie Gorman," I said, "You are the most evil, spiteful and miserable specimen of humanity I have ever met. But you know what, one day you're going to realise that, and then you'll have to spend the rest of your life living with yourself. That'll be fun."

"Hah!" Natalie retorted but we could see I had touched a nerve, and we left it at that and pushed through to the classrooms. Funnily enough she left us alone for a while after that.

Back home, Polly was still coming in every day to look after Dad, and Mum was still doing her 14-hour days.

"Polly," I said to her when I came home from school.

"Yes love," she replied as usual.

"Do you think Dad will ever play the piano again?"

"I don't know I'm sure, but it doesn't look like it, does it?"

"You know it's funny, but it wouldn't bother me now if he didn't. I mean he had his time at it, he became famous, he must have made a lot of money. It was great while it lasted but to be honest I'm actually quite glad it's over. That last tour of America would definitely have been too much for him."

"Yes, thank God he didn't have to go through with that," agreed Polly, "I suppose we should be grateful to that awful woman in a strange way."

"Yes, that was the best thing she ever did for him - destroying his career." And we both had a bit of a laugh.

"What does he do now all day?" I then asked Polly.

"Oh just sits in his chair in the family room mostly. I try to get him to do things - play games, look at picture books or the scrapbooks you put together, but he won't. He just sits there staring off into space again."

"It's not good for him that, is it?" I was getting concerned at what Polly was telling me. "If he just does nothing he'll go backwards and never get any better. He needs an interest in life. What can we do?"

"You're absolutely right girl, but what?"

"We'll have to think about it, and maybe draw up a list of things he could be doing. For a start he needs to get out more, maybe go to museums or galleries or places like that."

"You're right love. I'll think up a list and you do too, and we'll compare notes tomorrow. All right? But now I have to go."

"I'll ask Mum what she thinks when she gets home," was the last thing I said to Polly, but when Mum did finally come in the door, I took a look at her face and decided against it.

"What's wrong?" I asked her as soon as I'd got her dinner and a glass of wine on the table. I knew her well enough by now to know the minimum requirement for discussing what looked like bad news.

"Oh nothing for you to worry about."

"No please, tell me. A problem shared and all that."

"All right. Well you know Ms Bleating was going to sue us? Well she has, in an American court, and she has been awarded damages and compensation amounting to one million dollars."

"What? One million dollars! How?"

"You see when Papa didn't finish his concert in Carnegie Hall they sued her so she sued us to get it back. Then there was breach of contract for all the other engagements in the States that we pulled out of."

"But do they not know about Papa? Can they not see that he wasn't well? What kind of people are they?"

"They don't know anything about him. Oh there'll be

an appeal. This is just what they call a Summary Judgement. But we'll have to send over a team of lawyers and that will cost a fortune and meanwhile we have to lodge that amount in a what's called an Escrow account in America."

"Have we got that much money?"

"Just about, your father made quite a bit of money on his two tours, but it's going to clean us out."

"One million dollars! I can't believe it."

Just then I heard a noise and turning round I saw Dad standing in the doorway with a funny look on his face.

"Hello Papa," I said, going up to him and putting my arm through his. What do you want to do? Play in your bedroom?"

I turned him around to head upstairs but he resisted.

"No? Where do you want to go then?" And he started leading me through to this little room we have at the very back of the house overlooking the garden. Mum used to call it the study as it had Dad's old desktop computer and a printer in it though not very much else. Since we both have our own laptops now it hasn't been used for years, not since the last time Dad did his trading, the trading that Mum gave out yards about to Prof Meyerhofer in Austria a year earlier. It was cold and dark in there now, not having the radiator on, and the autumn sun had long gone down so I didn't really want either of us to stay. But Papa insisted on sitting down at the computer and I sat beside him and turned it on for him as that seemed to be what he wanted. When it finally warmed up I said, "OK so what do you want to do?" But he had it all sussed. He opened the Games file and then Solitaire and started playing away.

"Well you remember how to play that anyway don't you?" I said, and left him to it. An hour later I went to get him upstairs for bed and he was still there, playing Freecell this time, another card game he had always been fond of. He didn't mind when I told him he had to go to bed and turned off the computer.

The next day I came home from school again and Polly was sitting in the family room on her own.

"Hi Polly," I said, "Where's Dad?"

"He's in at that old computer in the study."

"Oh yeah, he made me bring him in there last night and started playing cards on it. Great, now he's become addicted to card games." I added sarcastically.

"Card games? Not at all, that's not what he's at."

"Well what then?"

"You come and tell me, I haven't got a clue." And Polly took my arm and we both went together past the kitchen and into the study. Polly had turned on the radiator in there so at least it wasn't so cold and it did have a lovely view out over the garden.

"What on earth is that then?" She said to me, pointing at the screen. "He's been at it all day. Won't stop for anything. What is that, all them squiggly black lines and squares and some straight red and blue lines. What does it all mean?"

"Oh that's his currency trading Polly. He started that a few years ago but he hasn't touched it since he had his accident. Mum says he was always useless at it but it's harmless enough. It's probably good for him in fact as it keeps the brain active, and we did need to find something for him to do, didn't we? He must have heard us! Let's leave him to it." So we made sure he was warm enough and comfortable and left him there, staring at his squiggly lines on the screen.

****

Autumn hung around till it had shaken all the leaves off the trees and life continued in its usual course of school, homework, occasional horse riding and drama. Polly and Dad were always there when I came home from school, sometimes with Sally, Mum coming home about eight o'clock for her dinner. And every day now, Papa would be at the computer when I came home. It was just like when he was playing the piano, it had become a complete obsession; there's no doubt but people in catatonic trances really get stuck into things.

Around this time Sally started worrying about her father again, because he'd started smartening himself up and being happy all over again.

"She must be back, this woman he's having an affair with," Sally was convinced, as she talked to me one evening on the phone. "He's taken to suddenly going out at night when he gets a phone call. Sometimes during the day. His phone rings, he answers it real quiet and he's off. How can I find out what's going on?"

"You could follow him," I suggested.

"I thought of that but he'd notice me. Would you come with me, you could keep a close tail on him coz he'd be less likely to recognise you, and I could stay behind a bit."

"'Keep a close tail on him'. You've been watching too many spy thrillers, you're beginning to sound like Jason Bourne. All right, but if we get caught it was all your idea, right?"

A few days later I was sitting at home doing my homework when my phone rang. It was Sally.

"I'm up on Hammersmith Bridge," she said. "He's heading down your road. They must be going to meet in Barnes. Can you leave the house in a few minutes, after he's gone past your gate and follow him? I'll stay back a bit and keep an eye on you. I'll ring again when it's safe to leave your house."

I told Polly I was going out for a while and with great misgivings about the whole plan I waited for the phone to ring.

"He's on the other side of the road and he's just gone past your house. You stay on your side and keep back a bit. I'll be able to see you. Go on, go now."

"Yes, Sally," I replied resignedly.

I went out the front door and down the drive and looked out the gate to the left, towards Barnes. Sure enough, there was Sally's Dad sauntering down Castlenau but whether he looked like he was going for a date I wouldn't have liked to say. He was wearing the new suit all right, but with a T-shirt and trainers, and he hadn't shaved, so he looked a bit odd really. I thought he was going to go down the high street but as soon as he got to the first shops he crossed the road onto my side which gave me an awful fright as I thought he'd be sure to recognise me when he checked for traffic. I stopped dead and looked into someone's driveway (fascinating) till he had crossed and was continuing on ahead of me. Then I realised where he was going - the public tennis courts and recycling place near the old reservoirs.

I followed him in at a safe distance and saw somebody else at the corner of one of the tennis courts who looked like they were waiting for their man. Only thing was, though, it wasn't his date. It wasn't even a woman, rather a dangerous looking young man with long hair dressed in the usual garb of the street. When they saw each other they looked around and then, at a mutual signal dodged in behind one of the big plastic bottle recycling skips. I looked behind me to see if Sally was anywhere near and was glad that she wasn't. So I decided to do the rest of the sleuthing on my own and I already had an idea of what was going on. I saw a half squashed 2-litre Coke bottle on the ground and, picking it up just in case I needed a cover, I walked casually round the other side of the skip. Wishing I had an invisibility cloak, I passed the end of it and took one quick look. Sure enough there the two of them were, exchanging money and plastic bags, though I couldn't see exactly which direction the trade was going in. I kept on walking and luckily they hadn't seen me. Then I had to get back to Sally as quickly as possible before her Dad came out again. I ran back to the entrance and saw her hanging round the junction. Crossing the road I said, "Come on, let's get out of here quick," and we walked down the High street a bit and ducked into the first shop we came to.

"What? What's going on? Did you see anything?" she asked, though I think she could see from my face that it wasn't going to be good news.

"Look out the door and see if you can see him," I ordered. Off she went and came back with, "He's just gone back up towards Hammersmith."

"OK, come on then." We both left the shop and walked round a bit, over towards the Common, while I told her what I had seen. We came to a bench and sat down together.

"I'm sorry, Sally, but I suppose, at least you know he's not having an affair."

"I wish he was now. At least you don't end up in jail for having an affair. How could he be so stupid? I know where he's getting the stuff. I heard him telling Mum once. Said there were guys in the airport who found drugs in bags and kept them, and if they bribed the security guy they could get them out of the airport. He must have gone in with these guys. Now he's selling the stuff on the street. My father's a drug dealer, I don't believe it Judy. What can I do?" And the poor girl put her head on my shoulder and started crying. She was my best friend, I had known her since we were eight, since our first day at school when we had walked in together through that enormous crowd, the two of us so small and so scared, and it broke my heart to see her like this.

****

As we came up to another Christmas, now a year and a half nearly since Dad had gone into his trance, it became harder and harder to go on believing that he would come out of it. There are all these sayings in life, like, "It's always darkest before the dawn" which are supposed to make you feel better, and give you hope, but they don't work, they're just stupid cliches, empty, meaningless words. The suits in the publishing company were right to tell me to avoid cliches. I hate them. But you still have to find some way to go on believing, and it's so hard. I know I told Mum once that it was easy to believe but it's not. Believing is the hardest thing to do in life.

Papa is a believer. Not the old Papa, he thought he was a complete failure, but the in-a-trance Papa. Once he stopped thinking that he could do nothing but fail, he suddenly found he could succeed. He did it with the piano and now, as I soon found out, he was doing it again with his trading.

One afternoon towards the middle of November I came home from school and found him as usual in the little study overlooking the now dusky, shadowy garden. I decided to sit down beside him for a while and watch. He had taught me a few things about trading three or four years before, when he started out, about what he called support and resistance. I remember how he explained it to me in a way that a child could understand. He said resistance is like the roof of a house, and the price keeps banging off it and can't get out. Then one day the price breaks up through the roof and because it is tired after all that exertion, it sits down on the roof again for a rest. That's support. Then it goes off again higher.

So as I sat there I tried to understand what he was doing, and looked at all the boxes of information on his screen. Some of them were easy to understand like date and amount, buy or sell, and profit or loss, and some were indecipherable abbreviations. Then I remembered him telling me once that he had £2000 in his account which he had put aside after selling his car and buying a cheaper one, and that was what he was trading with, very carefully so he didn't lose it all. I half knew where to find that figure, it was in a box called Account, under another heading I couldn't remember so I looked for it to see how much he had left. But I couldn't find any entry of around £2000 or less and began to think I was mistaken. There was an entry of £10,126 under the heading Balance all right, but that couldn't be right. I thought it must be a demo account but no, it said "Live" in red in the top right-hand corner. So I told Dad he had to go in for his tea, and after he'd made a few adjustments I brought him back to Polly. When I returned I sat down in his seat, opened up the full Trading Station and looked everywhere, and what I remembered from a few years ago came back to me. But there was no sign of any £2000 anywhere, just this figure of over £10,000 which, when I looked again, was now £10,525. There was no doubt about it, that was his current balance. But that was impossible, I told myself, he had only started trading again about five or six weeks ago, he couldn't have turned £2000 into over £10,000 in that length of time. Then I remember something else he had shown me before - how to get a statement of all trading activity over a certain period. It was called Report. I opened that file and there it all was, every trade he had ever made. Small losses and smaller gains from the earliest days up until September of this year, when the account stood at just under £1900. Then with no more than about twenty trades the balance had increased gradually, in hundreds and the occasional thousand, to where it stood today. Incredible. I hit the Print key and waited. Then I took the print-out and went up to my bedroom.

"Mum, what do you think of this?" I said to her that night after giving her her dinner.

"What is it? I can't read that, the print is too small."

"It's Dad's trading account, every trade he's ever made."

"Oh God, has he started that again? Why didn't you tell me? Well he can't do much damage I suppose as he has no money and cannot get his hands on any."

"Actually he has some money - look, £10,525 to be precise."

"Where did he get that?"

"He made it - trading. See - he started off with less than two thousand at the end of September and he's turned it into ten now."

"That's impossible, you can't make five times your money in a month and a half. There must be some mistake, you're looking at the wrong column or something - Oh God, has he lost ten thousand? Is there a minus in front of that figure? Show me. Oh God if he's lost ten grand on top of everything else I'll kill him."

"Mum, please, relax. It's not a minus number. It's OK."

"Well in that case it's one of those demo accounts, you know, a practice account."

"I checked that - it says Live Account up there in the corner, see?"

Mother finally calmed down and spent the rest of her dinner scrutinising the trading report, which, since she was an accountant by profession, should have been as easy as reading a Gary Larson cartoon. Thing was, she could understand it all right, she just couldn't believe it.

I, on the other hand, had no trouble believing it. After all, if he could play the piano now, I reasoned, why shouldn't he be able to trade successfully too? He was still working off the same subconscious part of the left side of his brain, as explained by Prof Meyerhofer. No fears, no hang-ups, no personal failure complexes, just pure mathematical calculations of risk-reward and probability, all done automatically.

The following morning I met Mummy in the hall as we were both heading out. She had the print-out in her hand and said, "I'm going to get my Head of Investments to look at this and see what he thinks," and she was off.

That night over dinner I finally had to ask: "Well? What did he think?"

"What did who think? Of what?"

"God, Mum, your Head of Investments guy, you said you were going to show him the print-out."

"Oh yes, I just gave it to him, he'll get back to me. Didn't tell him who it was of course." Grown-ups sometimes just amaze me. They have absolutely no sense of priorities, you know? They just don't know what's the most important thing in life at any one time. So I had to wait another twenty-four hours before I got an answer.

"Oh, right," said Mum over dinner the following night, "He said it's too early to tell, could be just luck and too much gearing," (that means too high a risk factor I should explain) "but to keep an eye on whoever was trading like this and in a couple of months I'd know whether to fire him or give him a large bonus."

A couple of months would take us up to after Christmas, I thought, I suppose I'll just have to wait.

"What about Christmas this year? Any plans on inviting some relatives round for drinks?" I asked mischievously.

"Yes, good idea, I think maybe some uncles and aunts -"

"No, no I was only joking, not your brothers again, please."

"Ha - got you! I just meant Uncle David and Auntie Anne."

"Oh that's all right, at least they're normal - no offence Mum but you know what I mean."

****

Christmas that year certainly was more normal than the previous one. No pressures of Dad's concert schedule to worry about, and no weird cousins and ever weirder uncles and aunts destroying the house on Christmas morning.

Uncle David and Auntie Anne and their three very normal children - Rebecca, Alison and John - came in for a while for drinks, and we all sat round the fire in the drawing room and had a nice chat. And because it was only them, we didn't need to get Papa out of the house, so we insisted that Polly spend the day with us instead and she was very happy to do so. The day went splendidly and I remember at the end of the meal, when I had eaten just about as much as I could take, looking around at my family, Papa at the head of the table where he belonged, Mum and I on either side, and Polly beside me, and saying, "You know we've come a long way together the four of us, I wonder what next year will bring."

And as if in answer, Papa immediately got up from the table and went into the study.

"Where's he off to - even he can't trade on Christmas Day," said Mum, "Go and see what he's up to Judy."

I followed him into the study where he had turned on the computer and was sitting in front of it waiting for it to warm up. It was cold in the little garden room so I didn't want him to stay long, but I sat beside him patiently and let him open up all the programs. The last one was his trading account and when I saw the current balance I was stunned - £50,963 as of the 24 December.

"Thanks Papa," I said, "Well done. Let's go back inside now." And he closed down the programs and turned off the computer and we both went back into the warmth of the dining room.

"I think he just wanted to show me," I said when we sat down again. "He's up to over fifty thousand, that's another five times more in the last six weeks."

"Great," said Mum, "If he keeps this up we can pay off the million dollars we owe." And we all looked at my father who was sitting there with a big smile on his face.

****

As it turned out we didn't need Papa to pay off the million dollars for us as we never had to pay it at all. Mum's lawyers went over to the States and fought an appeal and won. When the Appeal Judge heard about Papa's condition he overruled the previous award on grounds of ill-health, and we didn't have to pay anything to Ms Bleating or anyone else.

When we found out we were all delighted of course, but it didn't stop Papa continuing to trade as if his life depended on it. So much so, that by the middle of February he had made a quarter of a million pounds, and we were wondering what to do with the money. The Head of Investments in Mum's organisation had been asking about the mysterious trader and whether he had been fired or earned his bonus yet, and of course Mum had to go and open her big mouth and tell him who it was. So then it got all round her company, and pretty smartish it was all round the City, that there was a middle-aged man sitting at a ten-year-old home computer who wasn't exactly a candidate for Mastermind, but who was doubling his money every two to three weeks trading the Forex market.

And then it started all over again, like a recurring nightmare, only this time it was worse. When they found out that the financial wizard with the Midas touch was none other than their old friend, the piano-playing Chopinzee, the press had a field day, with headlines like "City Traders Go Bananas" and "How To Double Your Mon(k)ey" getting out before they were told to stop again. Then there were reporters ringing us up looking for interviews, bankers offering Dad a job trading for them, Fund Managers wanting in invest in him, the works. I couldn't believe it, that they had learned nothing from the previous experience, and now we had to go through it all over again, this time with people wanting Dad to make money for them. Talk about exploitation! Polly and I had no need to question it this time, this time there could be absolutely no doubt what was going on, but I was determined that nobody was going to exploit my father for financial gain. Nobody!

Nobody except perhaps Her Majesty's Government? I hadn't reckoned with that. This is what happened.

Remember the last of the Lunching Ladies, the one in the Rolls with the driver who should have offered her a piggy-back to the front door? Well, of course she found out about Papa, and you know her husband was a Government Minister, actually a Junior Minister in the Exchequer, so it wasn't long before we were honoured with another visit, this time from both of them.

They turned up in the Rolls again. Now everyone knows you can't afford a Rolls-Royce on the average Politician's salary; no, she had her own money from her family, and she had tons of it. And what do people buy when they have tons of money? They buy power of course. So Mum's friend, the honourable Lady Claudia Bassington-Smythe before she was married, bought herself a nice little slice of the Conservative Party in the form of Reginald Hardacre, MP for Grindsley-Northcup, and proceeded to groom him for Cabinet. And as I watched the two of them step out of the most expensive car in the world, which this time the driver had pulled right up to our granite front steps on Madam's side, I felt a cold chill run through me. They came into the drawing room and sat down with Mum while I went off to get the tea tray and boil the kettle with a feeling of deep foreboding. When I came back I couldn't believe what I was hearing from the Right Honourable Member for Grindsley-Northcup.

"... and so the Chancellor has asked me as a particular favour, to have a word with you and your husband, and to issue a personal invitation to you both, to meet Sir Roderick in Number Eleven at your convenience. And if his busy schedule allows, it is the intention of the PM himself to be there too."

"The PM himself," Mum murmured as if savouring the sound of those magical two letters.

"Indeed. The Prime Minister has expressed great interest in your husband's case and wishes to make himself available to you, should there be any grounds for future cooperation that would be mutually advantageous."

"That's a senior politician's definition of exploit-tation," I thought to myself, but, shame on me, I didn't have the nerve to say it. Actually I couldn't have said it or anything like it, it would have destroyed Mum. After they had their tea the three of them went in to see Papa who was safely ensconced in the family room again. I must say they were very nice to him and shook his hand and spoke to him directly and did everything in a way you would expect people like that to behave. Mannerly but oddly cold.

And then the farewells. We would be hearing from them. Back into the R-R, the footman holding the door open for Her Ladyship, while the politico actually managed to get into the car himself. And they were gone.

"Well Judy, what did you think of that?" said my mother as we went back inside. "That's exciting isn't it? Just imagine, the PM himself has taken an interest in Dad."

"Just imagine, the PM himself," I said with somewhat muted enthusiasm.

About two weeks later a letter arrived in the post with a rather natty seal on the back of the envelope. In spite of myself I couldn't wait for Mum to come home and open it. Strange the way we get when we think we're in the presence of Superior People - why is that? I just couldn't stop myself from getting excited. But if you think I was bad you should have seen Mum when she clocked the Chancellor of the Exchequer's headed 150-gram Vellum notepaper and Seal of Office. I thought she was going to kiss it.

"Listen to this:" she said, "'The Right Honourable Sir Reginald Perigrew Allweather, M.P., Chancellor of the Exchequer, requests the pleasure of the attendance of Mr and Mrs Jack Jones at a meeting at No 11 Downing Street on the 12th day of March. RSVP. Signed the Permanent

Undersecretary to the Chancellor of the Exchequer.' Sorry Judy you're not included."

"How will I ever live with the shame," I replied sarcastically though I really wanted to have been invited, but only to look after Papa's interests. Somebody had to, otherwise God knows what schemes they would concoct between the lot of them to make money out of my father. I had to think of something fast.

"Actually I really do want to go, and you have to get me invited. Tell them Dad won't go anywhere without his daughter, and that if they want him they will have to invite me too."

"Don't be ridiculous, they don't want a schoolgirl at their meeting, and why would you want to go anyway?"

"I need to be there, so I can tell my friends. Please Mum, tell them. Imagine the look on Natalie Gorman's face when I tell her I've been to No 11 Downing Street."

"All right Judy, I'll try, but I'm not promising anything."

"You have to write back to them anyway, it said RSVP didn't it? Please."

"All right. I'll try." And so, a week later, through the channels of communication that were now in place, it was made known to us that my presence at the meeting would be acceptable. They sent a car for the three of us and as we drove along the Embankment towards Westminster I kept repeating to myself, "Just make sure he's happy doing this, just make sure they don't try to use him, make sure he's OK doing it." But how I was going to stand up to the

Chancellor of the Excheck, not to mention maybe even the PM himself, I had no idea.

We arrived at the bottom of Downing Street, and stopped at those big gates Mrs Thatcher had put up to stop unwanted visitors, but as soon as the driver was recognised we sailed through and up past No 10 with its famous front door, and actually stopped right outside No 11. Then out of the car and in the big black door which magically opened just as we reached the front steps. Then we all got in a big lift which brought us up to the first floor where we were escorted into the biggest and grandest room I have ever seen in my life. It had four windows overlooking Downing Street, and a mahogany table about fifty feet long, in the middle of which sat my Mum's friend's politician husband and a couple of other splendid looking gentlemen, one of whom I recognised from the TV and papers when he did his annual pose for the cameras holding up what looked like his old lunchbox. This, I was aware, was the Chancellor of the Exchequer. The third man was introduced as the Permanent Undersecretary, which sounded uncomfortable, and I realised we were in the presence of Very Superior People.

We sat down, Mum, Dad, and me on one side of the huge table, and the three Very Superior People on the other. If this was to be a contest, to the average onlooker it must have appeared ever so slightly one-sided. The engagement commenced with our friendly politician explaining to the Chance that Mr Jones was the Private Equity Capital Trader everyone was talking about, (He's the what? I felt like asking) and explaining to us that we were all here to see if there were some way that we could cooperate to the benefit of all concerned. So the discussions went on, for about a half an hour, with the three boys doing most of the talking, Mum asking the odd question here and there, and me and Dad, not surprisingly, being pretty quiet. At the end of this time there seemed to be some kind of offer on the table whereby Dad would work for them, doing his trading, they would pay him a salary and give him a nice office somewhere, and the Exchequer would keep all of Dad's profits. Seemed reasonable. Queen and Country and all that. Actually her Majesty's name did come up on one occasion, it being suggested that Dad's trading prowess had come to the attention of the Palace, and that such service to the Crown and to her Majesty's Government as was being discussed, was generally met with Royal Approval.

With this irresistible hint hanging in the air I could see Mum ready to sign her life away, and mine and Dad's. I was trying desperately to think of some objection to make, and failing miserably, when suddenly the door sprung open and all hope of resistance was lost, for there in the flesh, advancing to meet us with hand outstretched was the ever-smiling, the ever-youthful, the ever-popular, the ever-so-handsome, the Right Honourable Member for Whitby, the Prime Minister himself, David Campbell.

The next ten minutes are, admittedly, a bit of a blur. All I remember clearly was a firm handshake, an irre-sistible smile and being swept along on a tide of patriotic euphoria until we found ourselves back out on the street, getting into the car again for our trip home, having signed my father over to the   Government to do with as they wished. Effectively we had said, "You can have him, do whatever you want with him, keep him as long as you like, use him for good or for ill, just send him back home on the bus to Barnes when you're finished with him." And we felt honoured to have been allowed to do so.

****

Chapter Nine - Papa Saves the Country from Financial Meltdown (Well, Nearly)

I must admit I woke up the following day asking myself, "What have you done?" and "How is this in Papa's best interests?" and "How were you blinded so completely by vanity and by the PM's flashy smile as to let those people make you happily sell your own father to them?" And a hundred other self-accusing questions, none of which I could answer. We had agreed, signed Papa up, and for the moment there was nothing we could do about it.

    A few days later we got word that a car would be sent to collect my father the following Monday morning to start his first day at his new job. We got him a 'Good Luck in your New Job' card and gave him a bit of a party on Sunday afternoon, but my heart wasn't in it at all. Polly was staying Sunday night with us and would go in with him in the morning before continuing on home, as Mum had to work and I had to go to school. He was to be finished at five and brought home again, but I decided I would get the bus into town after school and come home with him in the official car as I knew he didn't like getting into strange cars with strange drivers on his own. I could get some homework or study done on the bus. At least that was the arrangement for the first few days and we would see how he got on after that.

So first thing Monday morning, with an overpowering sense of *deja vu* all over again, I watched Polly and Papa get into the back of a big black car and crunch down our drive and out of our gate.

"At least they're not going too far this time," I said cheerily to Mum.

"Thank God that's over," she agreed. "What a song and dance his piano-playing career turned out to be. This will be much easier for all of us."

"I hope you're right." I replied wishing she didn't say things like that, you know, tempting fate. Fate must have absolutely no will-power at all, the slightest temptation and she gives in, usually with disastrous results for any humans involved.

That afternoon I went into town on the bus and walked over to Westminster. I had a phone number of some chap to ring who would meet me and together we would find Dad in the vast labyrinth of offices and corridors that is the Palace of Westminster, also known as the Houses of Parliament.

So I rang the number I had when I got to Big Ben, the only part of Westminster Palace I knew, and this nice chap who called himself DC Watson answered. I explained who I was and where I was and he told me where I should go. Ten minutes later, after getting lost a couple of times in swarms of tourists I met him at St Stephen's Entrance, the main entrance for members of the public, and we entered the building. As we went in he gave me an ID badge to wear around my neck which would get me in anytime I wanted. As I entered this vast, dark, cavernous building I felt like Bilbo Baggins entering the Lonely Mountain and wondered if I would ever see the light of day again. No exaggeration, it took longer to get from outside the Houses of Parliament to Dad's office on the fourth floor than it had taken on the bus into town. As we walked for miles along endless corridors of power and up and down long flights of stairs, I got to know my companion pretty well. He was Dad's driver, and in fact a policeman in disguise. I mean he wasn't wearing a uniform and Bobby's helmet, just a suit and tie. I asked him what kind of policeman he was and he said, "Oh just a lowly DC - that's Detective Constable for short." I resisted the temptation to comment on the obvious humour of being a detective called Watson which must have been pointed out to him on more than one occasion already.

"Are you going to be collecting your Dad every day Miss Jones?" said DC Watson, and I just loved the way he called me Miss Jones.

"For the first few days anyway, then we'll see how he is on his own."

"Right, in that case I'll show you where to wait tomorrow which will save you having to do this long haul."

"Sounds good to me," I said.

Eventually we found Dad's office, a big rectangular room with four large desks in it, one of which was Papa's and two of the others were occupied by a couple of young ladies. It also happened to have the most magnificent view over the Thames. Talk about right on the water, you could have leant out the window and spat into it if you were so inclined. I went over to Dad and gave him a hug as the

196

policeman introduced me to the ladies. "This is Mr Jones's daughter Judy," he said. "Judy, this is Stacey and Tracey."

"Oh, your Dad's really nice," they both said, "He doesn't say much, does he, but he's got a really nice smile." That reminded me of the air stewardess and I wondered had Dad been turning on the charm again with this pair.

"Bye Mr Jones," Stacey and Tracey said together, "See you tomorrow." And as I helped him up there was that dazzling smile again.

Out we went, and back along the endless corridors which, at Dad's pace took some patience, until we found ourselves in a lift heading down to the underground car park. Luckily the car was nearby, another big black affair with tinted rear windows. We all got in and pretty soon we were at the exit barrier.

"You see this corner here. If you just stand there at this time, quarter past five, tomorrow, I'll be able to pick you up, all right?"

"Great," I replied, "Now Papa, did you hear that? You're going to get in the car with the nice policeman tomorrow and come out here and pick me up. Then we'll go home together. OK?"

"Beggin your pardon Miss, and I don't mean to be offensive, but does he understand everything you say?"

"Yes he understands everything *everyone* says," I replied slightly pointedly, "He just doesn't respond. His brain functions perfectly in every way, but for some reason he chooses not to express anything himself."

197

"I know a few people I wish were more like your Dad," the driver said, "but will he ever come out of it, do you think?"

"Oh he'll come out of it all right, when he wants to."

"They say he's a financial genius," went on my friendly driver, "and he used to play the piano all over the world."

"That's right, all over the world," I said trying not to think of a certain concert hall in a large city in the US.

"That's amazing that is. Absolutely amazing. I hear he met the PM."

"Yes we all did, and the Chancellor."

"Oh he's boring, sorry shouldn't say that but he is. Don't suppose you'll tell anyone. But the PM, isn't he something?"

"Yes I suppose he is something," I couldn't help admitting.

"Much nicer than the last one, Browne - or Blair for that matter. Driven them all I have. I've been lucky, I'm only in the job six years but I've got to drive three PM's already."

"Great."

Pretty soon we were coming onto Hammersmith Bridge and as I looked out my window I caught sight of Sally's father heading down towards Barnes again. We passed right beside him on my left and I had to remind myself that he couldn't see me through the blacked-out windows. Same outfit as last time I saw him, same furtive look of someone up to no good, and a big bulge in his jacket pocket. The traffic was at a standstill on the bridge, and as we sat there I thought of something rather clever.

"DC Watson, have you got a badge?"

"Of course I have Miss."

"Can you do something for me, it's really important, you see this character on our left with the trainers and the stripy suit?"

"Yes Miss."

"Could you just open the window, show him your badge and tell him you know what he's up to and that you've got your eye on him."

"Well I shouldn't really. Miss, I could get into trouble, harassing members of the public. What is he up to then?"

"He's my best friend's father, and believe me, he's up to no good, and I have to give him a fright."

"OK, but this never happened right? What's his name?"

"Brown, don't know his first name."

"That'll do."

By this time Sally's father was nearly at the end of the bridge and a gap suddenly appeared in the traffic. DC Watson accelerated and then pulled into the curb as the electric window went down. I tried to hide in the corner and kept an eye out through the tinted windows.

"Oi you - Brown, I want a word with you," shouted the policeman out the window. I could see our friend's startled reaction, made a lot worse when he clocked the police badge that Watson was holding out to him through the window.

"We know all about you, Brown, got our eye on you we have. So watch it. What you got there?" We had both noticed him taking something out of his pocket as Watson was giving him the third degree. And then, as he backed towards the railings of the bridge we clearly saw him throw the package backwards into the river.

"I could have you for that," said Watson. "Next time you won't get away so lightly. And don't forget, we're on to you, right? So watch it."

We drove off and the last thing I saw through the rear window was Sally's father turning around disconsolately and heading back towards Hammersmith.

"Reckon we did the right thing there Miss, thank you very much. Intercepted and prevented a possible felony I'd say. Whatever he had in that package I don't know, but I reckon he wasn't on his way to Barnes pond to feed bread to the ducks."

When I got home I rang Sally and, without going into any details, was able to assure her that her father's career as a drug dealer was almost certainly at an end.

****

The next day worked out pretty much the same. Papa went into Westminster with the policeman while I went to school and Mum went to work. That was just like the old days, I reminded Mum, with the three of us going off in the morning. Then after school I got the bus into town and waited where DC Watson had shown me the day before, and sure enough he picked me up right at the agreed time.

He was a member of the Metropolitan Police Force, so I suppose he could be relied upon to keep good time. Then we drove home without any exciting incidents on Hammersmith Bridge or anywhere else. By the following day we all felt Dad would be fine on his own so from then on he travelled in and out to Westminster with DC Watson and I got on with my school life.

It was about six weeks later, as we were coming up to the end of term exams, that something interesting happened in school. The first anyone heard of it was when a Special Assembly was called one Monday morning at 11.00. Normally we had assembly first thing in the morning, as you would expect, to see if anyone hadn't managed to drag themselves in by 8.45. So Special Assembly was rare and, well, special. It meant you got off class for a start, but it usually meant that something interesting had happened, like one of the old nuns dying, so there's be a funeral and we'd get off more class. I don't wish to sound callous, but the nuns were all retired and rather ancient and these are the things that liven up life in the average Convent School.

Now the normal Morning Assembly is taken by Assistant Principal O'Leary or one of the senior teaching staff, but this morning as we trooped into the hall we were surprised to see the whole front bench up there, led by the Principal herself, Ms Dunstable. Oh oh, we thought to our-selves, this looks serious. As usual we started off with some prayers.

"In the name of the Father ..." Ms Dunstable led the way and we all followed like lambs of God. Then it was on to the main item on the agenda:

"Girls, something very serious has come to my attention. There has been the most serious possible breach of discipline, a matter which, when we discover the pupil responsible, will almost certainly result in her instant expulsion."

Well, this was most interesting, and got us all looking round at each other, agog. *Pray continue, dear lady, with your fascinating story* - the words of the Great Detective came to mind.

"You are all aware that the end of term exams are to commence in a weeks' time. The examination papers have been drawn up by all the relevant teachers at great expenditure of time and effort, and all papers have been delivered to my office where they have been under lock and key in my safe. However, on Friday evening, when I took the papers out of the safe to check something in one of them, I found to my utmost dismay that all of the examination papers for Year Three were missing."

At that point, I must admit, that old familiar feeling of rising panic did grip me, a feeling I had come to know only too well through the last two years with Papa. My immediate thought was that someone in our year was suspected - if not actually guilty - of stealing them. And I'd say everyone else in the school had pretty much the same idea. Ms Dunstable went on:

"At present we are conducting an internal investigation into the matter, and we hope that this will uncover the truth. My office has been thoroughly searched and has turned up only one page of one of the examinations involved. All other classrooms and other common areas are being searched as we speak. If this does not succeed, we will be forced to consider calling in the police. But before we resort to such extreme steps, which can only be detrimental to the reputation of our beloved school, let me make a personal appeal to whoever among you is responsible for this terrible act to examine your conscience, repent of your sin, and make a full confession. This is necessary not just for the well-being of the school and everyone in it, it is absolutely essential for the salvation of your own immortal soul. If, within the next two days, the person responsible comes to me, in private and in total confidence, restores the examination papers and makes a full and contrite confession, I assure you no further action will be taken. At the very least, if they cannot bring themselves to do that, an alternative course of action is open to them: leave the examination papers in the Chapel at some time over the next 48 hours. In this case however, I warn you all, that every effort will still be made to track down and punish the culprit. I will address you again in two days' time when I trust I will have better news to report. Meanwhile, may I see all of the Year Representatives in my office immediately after this Assembly. And now Ms O'Leary will lead us in singing the school hymn."

It was with many a suspicious glance around that the school hymn was rendered on this occasion. Ms Dunstable's startling announcement had made suspects and accusers out of all of us. I, as Year Rep, was getting more attention than most, with many a silent "Who do you think it was?" mouthed in my direction. At dismissal I obediently went straight up to the Principal's office where I joined the other five reps outside the door. When the Principal arrived, she unlocked the door, saying, "I am keeping this door locked at all times now, as we can sadly no longer afford to exercise the same degree of trust as hitherto." We then filed into the wood-panelled, carpeted office where we stood in a straight line in front of the Principal's desk. At least we tried to stand in a straight line but there wasn't enough room and there was a bit of jostling for space. The Principal came to the point.

"There is not much to add to what I said in my address. This is a terrible situation for all of us in this school. I look to the six of you girls, all of you chosen to represent your years because of your exceptional qualities of leadership and your stainless characters, to exert that leadership and moral strength, in making every effort possible to discover the truth. Talk to your peers, listen to what they are saying, examine every rumour and accusation fairly and with good judgement, and if you find out anything that may be relevant, report it back to me. God bless you all. You may go now. Except you Judy if you please."

When the others had gone I was invited to sit down opposite the Principal which was quite an honour.

"Judy, my dear girl, you have had a lot to bear over the past two years with the illness of your father, not to mention the extraordinary events that have occurred in the lives of you and your family. I have watched you dealing with these trials with great interest and admiration, and it has been made clear to me that you are a person of the finest qualities of intelligence, integrity, loyalty and courage. As it is your year whose examination papers have gone missing, naturally the suspicion must fall upon your classmates to a greater degree. If there is anything you can do to bring this matter to a satisfactory conclusion we will be eternally grateful. You may go back to class."

"Thank you Principal," I replied, genuinely touched, "I will do my best." Then something occurred to me. "Do you mind if I ask you a question?"

"Anything at all my dear."

"You said in your address that one page of one of the papers had been found. Where was that page found?"

"Right here, on my desk. I must have been looking through the Year Three papers earlier that day and left them on my desk. All the others were locked in the safe. Then I must have been called away for some reason and when I remembered later on what I had been doing, and looked for the papers on my desk they were all gone, except for one page which I had separated from the rest."

"And what page was that?"

"It was the first page of the English paper, which Mr Rogers had just finished and delivered to me."

"So how long was the office unoccupied with the papers on the desk?" I felt we were getting somewhere now and was enjoying using my best Sherlock Holmes style of questioning. Anyone who hasn't read the Holmes stories really ought to, as they are great.

"Perhaps an hour, it's difficult to say. You see, my dear, sometimes I lose track of the time, you know at my age, one does."

When she said this I looked at her for possibly the first time not as the figure of authority which she had been to me since my first day in the school as a scared little eight-year-old. I saw her now as she really was, a frail, elderly lady trying to cope with a very difficult situation, not helped by the fact that her mental powers were diminishing and her memory wasn't as good as it really needed to be.

"Was anyone else around?"

"I don't think so."

"But it was Friday - what about the cleaning lady?"

"Oh Mary was here all right, but she'd never ... she's been with us for years. No it was definitely one of the girls, but you may go back to class now."

"Yes Principal."

****

You can imagine the uproar in the school and especially in my year after this announcement. And being schoolgirls, who have a tendency to be a little, how shall I put this politely - *bitchy* - we all had the time of our lives with accusations and counter-accusations flying everywhere. I listened to them all and ignored most of them, but one name kept cropping up, one name was the chief suspect on everyone's lips, and that name was Natalie Gorman. Not that anyone felt she needed to cheat, but just because she was the only one, as she had shown in the previous year's Christmas tests, who would dare perform such an outrageous act. I couldn't wait to get home to discuss the scandal with Polly and Mum.

"Natalie Gorman of course," said Polly as soon as I gave her the facts and asked who she thought did it. "She's cheated before so she's the most likely one to have done it again. Stands to reason, doesn't it?" Mum's view was slightly different.

"From what I've seen of the nuns and teachers in that school of yours, they've probably just lost them. One of them has used the exam papers to light a fire, or she's shredded them and given them to the cat for cat-litter, or something. They'll probably never turn up but that doesn't mean they've been stolen. Why would anybody steal them anyway - once the teachers realise they're missing they have to rewrite the papers so they're of no value to anyone. Doesn't make sense."

"I know, I thought of that. The only way would be if someone could make a copy and get them back before it was noticed they were missing."

"And where's the photocopier?"

"In the Secretary's office, but she's usually there."

"Too risky. No schoolgirl is going to run the risk of getting in and out of the Principal's office, and the Secretary's office, using the photocopier while she's there, and then back to the Principal's office again. That's madness."

Two days later, when no-one had admitted the crime, not even for the salvation of their eternal soul, and the papers hadn't appeared in the Chapel or anywhere else, I was beginning to think Mum was right and Ms Dunstable had just lost them herself. I would have been inclined to leave the matter except that it had such a bad effect on our class. The rest of the school started making nasty comments about Year Three being thieves and cheats and we started fighting among ourselves and accusing each other to such an extent that something had to be done to prove none of us was guilty. It even got too much for Natalie Gorman who came up to me in the yard one lunchtime and said:

"Listen Jones, you probably think I'm the one who pinched those papers don't you?"

"Actually I don't but maybe I'm wrong. Was it you?"

"No it bloody well was not and I'm getting a bit tired of everyone accusing me. You've got to do something about it, Jones, you're class rep, Dunstable trusts you, you've got to tell her it wasn't me and get her to make an announcement or something. You know, get everyone off my back."

"As usual all you care about is yourself. If everyone believes you did it it's because you've got yourself such a bad reputation and it serves you right. However I do intend getting to the bottom of this and when I do you will be cleared, but I'm not doing it for your sake. Now if you'll excuse me I'd like to finish my lunch in peace."

I had one more idea I wanted to put to Ms Dunstable so I went up to the Secretary as soon as I was finished eating to see if I could see her boss. They were both in the Principal's office and when she saw me I was invited in.

"I am afraid we are none the wiser since our last meeting Judy, I am beginning to believe we will never find out what happened to the papers. The Board has decided not to pursue matters with the Police." A vision of fire-lighting and cat-litter came to mind which I tried to dismiss and asked instead:

"Can I make one suggestion please?"

"Any help you can give us would be greatly appreciated my dear."

"My father is doing some work for the Government at present, and he is being driven in and out of town by a Detective. Would you mind if I had a word with him, in confidence, unofficially, and see if he has any ideas. He's very nice and very clever."

"Yes I think that would be all right, as long as it was all kept quiet."

"Oh absolutely, he's very discreet."

"Would he want to come into the school?"

"Perhaps, but that would be no problem. You see he's a plain-clothes detective so no-one would know he was a police officer."

"A plain-clothes detective! How exciting!" That had obviously sparked some notions in the old dear's head.

"Well thank you my dear and do let me know if you discover anything."

"Yes Principal, goodbye." And as I stood up the chair caught in the carpet and I nearly fell over backwards, most embarrassing. I went back to class and on the way I started thinking. By the time I got to my desk I had a pretty good idea of what had happened and who was responsible.

But there's only so much a 15-year-old Sherlock Holmes can do on her own - it was time to call in Watson.

That afternoon I went into town and rang DC Watson to pick me up outside the car park. On the drive home I told him all about the case and got his opinion, and he agreed to accompany me into school the following day at nine o'clock and to bring Papa into work a bit later on.

So the following morning I entered the school gates and crossed the yard in the company of my handsome young Police Detective. Of course no one had a clue who he was and it caused some comments I can tell you. We went straight up to the first floor and asked to see the Principal and were shown straight in.

"Principal Dunstable, this is the Detective I was telling you about, Detective Constable Watson. He's here to help us deal with the culprit. But first we need to find those missing papers."

"Of course my dear, but no one knows where they are, do they?"

"We shall see," I replied and gave my new colleague a nod.

"You say this room has been locked ever since you discovered the loss?" asked Watson.

"Yes that's right."

"And there is no possibility that anyone has been in here alone during that time?" Watson again.

"No, none whatsoever."

"In that case," me this time, "The papers should still be right here in this room."

"But that's impossible, the whole office has been searched, turned upside down."

"Except," I said, "For one place -" I went down on my hands and knees at the corner of the desk and started feeling the carpet. After a minute I found what I was looking for, a tear in a seam about four inches long at the corner of the desk, just wide enough to fit a small hand. I slipped my hand in and with a dramatic flourish pulled out the folded up examination papers.

"I think this is what we have been looking for," I said and placed them on the Principal's desk. "And now we need to interview Mary the cleaner."

Well the excitement! The secretary was called in and then some teachers heard and they came in, and Ms Dunstable kept saying, "Judy's found the papers, they were in the carpet, Judy found them." And DC Watson looked really pleased, and everyone kept saying, "How did you know?" so I had to explain how I had worked it out.

"You see I never believed from the start that any of the girls was responsible, partly because of something my Mum said, that they couldn't have got away with it and the papers weren't worth stealing anyway because you would just rewrite them; and partly because of the attitude of my classmates: no-one seemed to know anything about the theft. Then when I heard one of the pages was left on the desk I knew they had been grabbed in a hurry and probably hidden. The only person around at that time was Mary the cleaner, so I reckoned she must have seen them on the desk and taken them, hoping to get them photocopied and return them before they were missed. She would have a much better chance of using the photocopier while in the office cleaning, than any of us. But before she could leave the office she was disturbed by the sound of someone in the corridor, and she needed a place to hide them quick. She would have been the only person aware of a tear in the carpet that could be used for this purpose - she must have noticed it a hundred times going over it with the vacuum cleaner. I suppose she thought she could get them later but never got the chance, as the room has been kept locked ever since. I had noticed how old the carpet was when my chair caught in it the last time I was here. Then I remembered the morning after Assembly when all the Year Reps stood in a line in front of the desk. One of the girls must have tripped over an unevenness in the carpet as we all kind of bumped into each other. She must have been standing here, right on the hidden exam papers. The only thing I don't understand is why Mary would do it and how she hoped to profit from the theft. But since today is Friday she should be coming in again later and perhaps with the help of my friend Doctor - I mean DC - Watson, we can find out."

When the cleaner turned up for work she was duly interviewed and admitted the theft, and it all turned out to have been pretty much as I had said. She had hoped to get the papers photocopied before they were missed and to sell the information to one or other of the rich girls in the class. You see she needed to make a bit of money to get her husband out of a spot of money bother he was in with his bookie. Watson offered to cuff her and take her away forthwith but the Principal took pity on her. Since she was so happy to have the matter cleared up she let the cleaning woman off with a stern rebuke from representatives of both School and Law Enforcement.

Then we had to have another Special Assembly at which Ms Dunstable gave me more praise than I deserved and I'm certainly not going to repeat any of it here, but which went down pretty well with my classmates. Even the bold, the brazen and now the bashful Natalie Gorman came up to me afterwards and said, "You're all right Jones, you know that, you're all right." After seven years, Gee thanks Natalie.

****

Writing this book has turned out to be harder than I had at first imagined. I've just realised I have been going on about myself and my school life for the last twenty pages when I should have been telling you about Papa. I mean it is his story I'm supposed to be telling, not my own. So when the mystery of the missing exam papers was cleared up we had our exams and pretty soon we were into the summer holidays. That gave me the chance to spend more time with Papa and, since I got on so well with my Detective Constable, I started going into town with the two of them some days, spending the day going round the shops or meeting my friends and then getting a lift home again after Dad had done his day's grind of making money for H M's Govt. Occasionally if I had time to kill I would go into Papa's office in the afternoon and talk to the girls, or sit beside him and watch, or just look out the window at that incredible view of the river till the time came when he could punch the clock and leave.

It was on one of these last occasions, when I was just sitting quietly at the end of the room at the spare desk looking out the window, and Stacey and Tracey had gone out to get coffee, so there was just Dad there on his own, that I witnessed something that made me realise I had been right to have serious doubts about this business. As I said, I was sitting right down at the end of the room and the desk I was at had a stack of filing trays on it, when these two characters came in. I could sort of see them through the filing trays though I couldn't identify them. They obviously hadn't seen me and weren't expecting anyone else to be in the room. So I stayed hidden and this is what I heard.

"How's he doing then?"

"Pretty good."

"What's he trading?"

"Euro-Dollar, Cable and ... Dollar-Swiss looks like."

"Can he hear us?"

"Naw, he's deaf and dumb. Never opens his mouth. See - nothing." And one of them waved his hand up and down in front of my father's face.

"Does he trade anything else apart from currencies?"

"No, just currencies."

"What's he up to now?"

"About five hundred million. We were taking a few million off the table every week at first just to be on the safe side, but now we're just letting it run. "

"What's his turnover, percentage-wise?"

"Unbelievable. Between four and five hundred per-cent."

"Four to five hundred percent a year? That's pretty damn good."

"Not a year - a month!"

"What?! Four to five hundred percent a month? That's impossible!"

"I know. I know it's impossible, but that's what he's doing."

"If he was making fifty percent a month it'd be impressive, but five hundred?"

"I know, tell me about it, that's why he's in here."

"Right. PM wants this optimised. Give him another five hundred."

"Five hundred thousand?"

"No. Five hundred million. We have to get him up to ten billion before the end of the year. We all know the US Banks are going down, and ours will follow. We're going to need every penny we can get our hands on and this guy's going to help us make it. So sit on him."

"With all my weight."

With that they both laughed and left. I gave them a minute and then went up to my Dad where he sat quietly at his desk and gave him a hug. When the two girls came back in with their coffees I was back in my chair at the other end of the office.

The following day I went into town with Papa and DC Watson again, and when we got there I asked him could I have a lift home at the usual time.

"Sorry Miss, no can do."

"Why not? Are you not on duty?"

"No it's not that, it's just that your father has to work a bit later than usual tonight."

"Oh - why - how late?"

"My orders are to collect Mr Jones at nine o'clock. I know it's late and I'm sorry, but that's my orders."

"Nine o'clock! But that's much too late for Dad. He needs to get home and have his dinner. How will he survive?"

"Don't like it much myself Miss, but orders is orders. I heard them discussing it, and I think they want him working on until the markets close in New York, that's nine o'clock our time, that's what I was told."

"New York again," I thought, "What is it about that place?"

"And who exactly decided that, do you know?"

"Sorry Miss, even if I knew I couldn't tell you. Security and all that."

But I knew already from what I had overheard in Papa's office where these orders were coming from. Those two gentlemen were obviously very high ranking. The first one was probably David Campbell's private secretary and the other was some kind of Investments chief. They clearly meant to keep Dad working like a slave until he had made them enough money to get them out of whatever mess the economy was in. Their orders were coming right from the top, from the Prime Minister himself, and there was nothing I could do about it.

Or was there? I had to do something, I couldn't let them treat Dad like a slave. That afternoon I went back into Westminster and entered Parliament Buildings without any difficulty thanks to my security pass. Ten minutes later I was up in Dad's office where I found him working away at his desk with the girls at the other desks.

"I'm just taking my Dad for a bit of exercise," I said to the girls, "Just up and down the corridor, stretch his legs like."

"All right love, ta-ra then."

"Come on Papa," I said, and as soon as we got out of the office, added, "We're getting you out of here right now." But the words were no sooner out of my mouth when two rather large men in suits came around a corner and walked straight into us. One of them I recognised from yesterday, the one I had identified as Investments boss. The other was a bit of a bruiser in a Security Guard uniform.

"Where do you think you're going old man, and who the hell are you?" said the first one.

"How dare you speak to us like that," I said," And if you have to know, I am Mr Jones's daughter and I'm taking him home."

"That's what you think, back inside, now, both of you." said the other member of this comedy duo. "We're under orders to make sure he stays at his desk and does what he's supposed to do. What'll we do with her?"

"She can stay if she behaves herself, I suppose."

"Right, you can stay here today, but that's the last time you get in, here give me that." And this animal grabbed my security ID and pulled it over my head.

"Ow, that hurt," I said, but I didn't want to make too much of a fuss because of Papa. Even so, I heard him start to make some familiar noises, the meaning of which I knew only too well.

"What's his problem?" asked the Security Guard. "What's with the Ape-man routine?"

"Didn't you know? You've been detailed to look after the Monkey Man himself," said the other, and when Papa heard that name the noises got worse.

"How dare you speak of my father like that." I exclaimed. "I'll have you both fired, I know the Prime Minister." If I thought this was going to impress them I was disappointed.

"So do we Miss, so do we. Now inside."

When we got into the office the men seemed surprised to see the two girls working there, as they hadn't been there the day before. That made them change their tune a bit.

"Now I'm sure you'll be very comfortable here until it's time to leave," the Investments guy said, "I'm sorry you have to work late tonight Mr Jones but it won't be for long and we can get you anything you want for your dinner from the canteen. Now if you don't mind I'm going to leave you in the hands of my colleague here who will attend to your every need." Then he left us with the Minder keeping an eye on us from a seat by the door.

I didn't want to say anything in front of the girls so I just made sure Papa was all right and got him back to work, and then I went and sat down at the spare desk. But there was no doubt things were taking a turn that I was not happy with and I needed to get Papa out of there before the situation got worse. Without my security pass I had no way of getting back in again in future so it had to be done now. But how could I with that bouncer at the door?

When six o'clock came I had a bit of a plan.

"Excuse me," I said to our friend, "My father will be getting hungry now so if we could go down to the canteen and get something to eat we would appreciate it." The bouncer thought for a minute and then said:

"My orders are you stay right here. He has to go on working till nine o'clock. If you want something I'll get it." What is it about these people and orders? I thought, do they ever do anything without being ordered? Then he went and whispered something to the girls. When he came back he looked satisfied.

"Steak and chips all right?" he asked me. "I'll get you both steak and chips if you like. They do a good steak and chips in the canteen so they do."

I could see which way his thoughts were running and saw a possible way out. "Sounds great," I said, "Hurry up won't you, we're starving. I mean you're not going to stay down there and have your own dinner are you?"

"What's it to you if I do?" he replied indignantly, "I'll stay as long as I like," and I knew I had plenty of time. He was practically rubbing his tummy and licking his lips as he went out the door.

"What's he on about?" said one of our female companions, Stacey I think it was, when he left. "Tellin us to keep an eye on you and not let you out of our sight."

"Who does he think he is, I'd like to know, " agreed Tracey. "So Stace, you comin home then?"

"Sure am Trace, see you tomorrow Mr Jones, see you tomorrow Miss Jones." And the two lovely young ladies gathered up their belongings and went out.

"Right, now's our chance, come on Papa, let's go." But he wouldn't leave his desk or even stop working.

"Papa, come on, we don't have much time." Still he wouldn't budge, but went on frantically hitting keys and opening and closing pages on his screen.

"Please Papa come on, we have to get out of here before he comes back. You don't need to do any more work for them. It's over, you've done enough." Finally I got him to finish what he was doing and come with me but we'd lost a lot of time. We went straight out to the lift we always use as I thought the best way out was the quickest. We made it into the lift all right and pressed the ground floor button, but as soon as the doors opened I knew we'd made a mistake. I could see a big crowd of security men at the main entrance and the Investments guy was there too. I immediately pressed the button again for the top floor but we'd been spotted. Nevertheless as the lift went straight up to the top without stopping at any other floors I reckoned we had a bit of time. I remembered from the first day how to get to the other set of lifts which took you to the car park in the basement so I got Papa over there as quickly as possible and we called the lift. As we waited I took out my phone and rang DC Watson. He answered straight away.

"DC Watson," I said trying to sound calm, "It's Judy Jones here. Hi. My father and I would like to leave now and I wonder if you might meet us in the car park to take us home."

"Of course Miss Jones, I can meet you at the bottom of the lift in about five minutes." That sounded hopeful but there was something in his voice that made me wary. He had told me earlier he was leaving at nine and he was after all a policeman so he was absolutely not going to disobey orders for a 15-year-old girl. I didn't like it. The lift came and the doors opened. I thought for a minute. Then I reached in, pressed the emergency stop button and took Papa's hand and started walking in the other direction. We had to find some way out but they were obviously looking for us by now so all the exits would be blocked.

We were now on the very top floor of the Palace of Westminster, and I had absolutely no idea how to get out. I knew there wasn't much they could do to us if they caught us, I mean they couldn't lock us up in the Tower of London or cut off our heads. I just didn't like the way they had treated Papa and wanted shot of the place.

So we kept on going and as soon as we reached the end of this top corridor we saw DC Watson and a number of others including the security guard come out from the main staircase and head after us. There was no way out of there so I resigned myself to being caught and brought back. Wouldn't be too bad, there was always the steak and chips, I thought. We were standing at the very end of the corridor in the furthest corner beside a window, and I noticed there was scaffolding outside. Papa was at the window and I was wondering what he was doing when suddenly, just before the posse caught up with us, Papa

221

pulled the window open. Looking past the scaffolding I saw a drop of about two hundred feet to the ground below, a large triangular lawn called, as I found out later from the news reports, College Green. Well I'm not going out there, I thought, but Papa had other ideas. He grabbed my hand and pulled me out the window until we were standing on a platform made up of the usual planks of wood not very securely tied down that workers have on scaffolding. The scaffolding was there, I also found out from the TV news, for the purpose of the stone restoration program which had been going on for some years. I was petrified and couldn't move but Papa somehow came into his element and started on down to the next level which was accessed by a shaky ladder. I had no choice but to follow him down. And then on down to the next level. I looked up and noticed we weren't being followed - they had more sense. Twenty levels of scaffolding in all, I know because I counted each one.

By the time we were about halfway down we had attracted a crowd of onlookers below, among whom, as far as I could see without falling, was a number of policemen's helmets. And still Papa went flying on down. At one stage, about six levels from the ground, he actually went out on the scaffolding itself and started shinnying down it like a ... like a ... well, like a monkey if you really must know. And from there to the ground he didn't bother with the work-men's dodgy ladders, he just used the scaffolding itself. Well I'll tell you that really got the crowd going, and when we reached the bottom they let out an almighty roar. The local constabulary weren't so impressed and offered to escort us off the Green to a waiting police car. With a wave to the crowd, Papa got into the car with the biggest smile I've ever seen on his face. I think he really enjoyed that; it brought out his true inner nature.

The next few hours were admittedly a bit of a mess, having to explain ourselves to countless numbers of police and other officials, until someone from No 11 came and sorted it all out and we were allowed go home. By then of course it had been on all the news programs as numerous phone cameras and video cameras had been pointed in our direction coming down the scaffolding, and our fame had spread throughout London. "Monkey Man climbs down Westminster Palace" shouted all the headlines, and this time it was really pretty pointless to complain.

"What in the name of God were you two doing?" My mother asked as soon as we rolled up in the police car. She was a bit cross and quite justifiably so for once I must admit.

"You're on every news bulletin and radio station in the country. I was in the office when someone spotted you on the Internet. I don't normally expect to have my day's work interrupted by the sight of my husband and daughter doing a Tarzan and Jane impersonation on the front of the Houses of Parliament."

Poor Mum, she was a bit upset, so I got her another drink and made her a nice dinner, and Papa and I settled down for the rest of the night to watch ourselves a few more times on TV. That was the first time he had ever actually watched anything on TV in two years, and do you know what, I think he really enjoyed it.

Mum came in and put Papa to bed, telling me not to stay up too late but there was a movie on that I wanted to watch so I sat there on my own. Now I never fall asleep in front of the TV but I suppose I must have been tired with all the excitement of the day (not surprising really) and suddenly in the middle of the movie I found myself back in the monkey house of the Zoo with Papa in front of me in his glass cage. He was smiling and talking as usual but as usual I couldn't hear or understand what he was saying. Then I noticed something funny about him. He was wearing a suit and a bow-tie and the trousers were short. Then I looked behind him and there was a long table with a number of chimpanzees sitting at it, all dressed in real clothes, suits for the male chimps and little dresses for the females. As I watched, a zookeeper entered the cage from the rear and took Papa's hand. I felt elated, believing that he was going to take Papa out and give him back to me but instead he brought him up to the table and sat him at the top where he joined in with what was now clearly a Chimpanzees' Tea-Party. I started shouting and screaming at the zookeeper to give me my father back but of course I was ignored. A crowd gathered round to watch the tea-party and they all started laughing at the antics of the chimps. I couldn't take any more, it was so humiliating and heartbreaking to see my father there like that, and for the first time I just wanted to leave him there. I turned away and walked out of the monkey house into the bright daylight outside and woke up. In all the time since he fell ill I had never felt such despair, and for the first time I gave up hope of ever getting Papa back again. "Why? Why?"

was all I could say. I didn't understand anything - the illness, the trance, the dreams, I had always believed I would find a way to release my father from his dreadful catatonic state but everything seemed more hopeless than ever. And the image of him with the chimpanzees was so degrading it tore my heart out and yet I couldn't get it out of my head. There was something nagging at me, trying to get me to understand, something Prof Meyerhofer had said about the chimpanzees' tea party ... eventually I remembered - "Perhaps it might be the key we are looking for to understanding your father's condition," he had said. And then I had an idea. I decided to ring the Professor and tell him about my dream.

****

Chapter Ten - Papa Attends Another Chimpanzees' Tea Party

After his rather public display of my father's determination to resign from the employ of Her Majesty's Government, the Chancellor and the PM had no choice but to accept his portfolio, as they say in Whitehall. I had no regrets and still felt that Papa had been badly treated until it transpired that he had effected a perfect revenge. Remember when I couldn't get him to leave the office when the security guard had gone off for his steak and chips? Well you'll never guess what he had been up to. He was placing one last trade, a complicated type of trade call a Contract for Difference, to buy an Call Option on the FTSE Financial Index. Now this index was falling like a stone, and Papa knew it was going to continue to fall, so he had exposed the Government to a potentially limitless loss since his position was to buy £100 million worth of the index.

Over the course of the next few days word of this huge losing trade got out and it was the talk of the City. One of the main banks was making big money out of being the counterparty to Papa's trade but no one knew who had taken the opening position. All they knew was that it originated from a computer in the Palace of Westminster and of course the Government wasn't going to admit anything. Someone was now sitting at Dad's computer desperately trying to get out of this position and lose as little as possible, but in the end the final loss for the government was revealed to be in the region of £500 million - exactly the figure, funnily enough, that Papa had already made for them. So that put an end to Papa's short career as a rogue trader.

It was at this time that Bill, my agent, came into our lives. I had noticed him among the crowd when we had come down off the scaffolding - you couldn't miss him as he was so tall and had so much hair. He had even managed to slip me his card between our coming out of the police station where he had followed us, and getting into the car. Then the following day he rang us up, apologising for the call but saying that he got our number from the press office in No 10 Downing Street. That made him sound pretty well connected, Mum thought, so we let him come over to the house and talk to us about how he could protect us from the rest of the press, and best serve our interests. We both liked him and it just sort of took off from then. Amazingly, after that, the reporters left us alone, and the only calls we got were from Bill, saying is it OK to say this and what would we like to say about that. And everything appeared n the press just the way we wanted it to. How he did it we had no idea.

****

We were now into the month of August, and coming up to exactly two years since Papa went into his trance. Ever since Munich I had been keeping in touch with Professor Meyerhofer by email, which at times really took some doing as Papa seemed to be living quite an exciting life.

Although since the end of his trading career things had thankfully quietened down, and the only excitement he ever got now was the odd trip to Ikea. But after our phone conversation I was expecting to hear from him and one day I got an email from the little old Professor which was to change everything. He wanted us to come over to Austria again as he said he had set everything up for the treatment which we had discussed and he really thought it might help Papa. I got really excited at this prospect but Mum of course reacted quite differently when I told her over dinner.

"Now don't go getting your hopes up darling. It will probably not come to anything. Why did he have to say that, you'll just get disappointed when it doesn't work."

What is it about grown-ups that makes them so negative all the time? They're always expecting the worst. What are they afraid of? I think they believe if they hope for something good, God will whack them over the head and say, "No you can't have that and don't dare ask again!"

"Mum, I'm not getting my hopes up. If it doesn't work it doesn't work, but can't we at least give it a go and hope for the best? Go and look up the flights and let's get over there as soon as possible. Oh won't it be great for the three of us to be flying to Salzburg again? Just like old times!"

Mum finally agreed and booked the flight for a week later, a direct flight to Salzburg. And it wasn't first thing in the morning so we didn't have to get up in the middle of the night like the last two times, although we still ended up at the back of the plane as we were the last to check in as usual. But at least the three of us were together in our favourite seats, me at the window, Mum on the aisle and Dad in between. As we took off this time I held Papa's hand so tight it must have hurt and prayed and prayed that our plan would work and Papa would be cured and come back to us again. It was too late for breakfast so I ordered some sandwiches which we ate together while Mum had her usual coffee and bun.

The Austrian countryside with its scenery of lakes and mountains was as beautiful as ever, and this time I could enjoy it as we drove in the taxi from Salzburg out to the lake. We had been through so much together, the three of us, since we took that first trip back home from the hospital, and we had survived, and Papa was getting better all the time.

We got to our apartment and Mum started to unpack while I took Papa over the old iron footbridge to the supermarket on the other side of the river. As we crossed together I looked at the sunlight shining on the water and remembered the last time we had followed this route, the very first morning after Papa came out of hospital. I couldn't believe how much had happened in those two years, how much my father had achieved in such a short period of time and under such extraordinary circumstances. And as I held his hand and helped him down the steps at the far end of the bridge I realised how we had done it - one step at a time, just taking everything as it came to us.

"Just one more step, Papa," I said as we headed for the supermarket, "Just one more step and we'll be there."

When we got home with the groceries Mum had finished unpacking and was ready to go to the hospital.

Professor Meyerhofer had said to just call in whenever we arrived. We ordered a taxi because it was too far for Papa to walk, and on the way over Mum asked about what the Professor had said and wondered what his new treatment might possibly involve.

"Whatever he has in mind I can't imagine," she mused. "It must be some new drug, I suppose, or some form of psycho-therapy, or maybe even hypnosis, or ... "

****

"... A Chimpanzees' Tea Party?!"

"Ya, that is what I have said. Your daughter Judy gave me the idea from her dream. We are going to organise for your father a repeating of the Chimpanzees' Tea Party which he was enjoying in the Zoo when he was a child. We are having all the chimpanzees coming here from our scientific laboratories in Vienna. They are very special chimpanzees we are using for our studies there, very intelligent animals are these, and very well looked after."

Mum and I were back in Professor Meyerhofer's office for this revelation, and my father was with one of the nurses well out of earshot, which was just as well.

"What I believe is," he continued, "That your father suffered a severe psychological depression when he was in the apartment on his own during the month of August two years ago. That acute negative mental condition caused him to revert to the first great psychological trauma of his life, when he was between eight and ten years old and having his birthday parties in the Zoo, and his normal personality

230

was taken over by the self-image he hated most. There were many influences which made your father sub-consciously choose this monkey or chimp persona. First there was the name calling in the school, with the nickname Monkey Face. Then the singing of the Happy Birthday song with the words changed to say he looks like a monkey. Then there was the extremely traumatic occurrence when the zookeeper handed your father the chimpanzee and it bited him. All these elements - though they happened at different times - converged in your father's mind on that day and caused him to become this monkey persona. It is the way of the subconscious mind to deal with a form of stress that the conscious mind is not strong enough to withstand. But if we go back to that point in his childhood and recreate this traumatic experience in a controlled experiment, I believe there is a chance that his subconscious and conscious minds will come back into equilibrium. So it is my belief and my hope that if we repeat these experiences of childhood that your father will revert to being himself again. We shall see."

This re-enactment was planned for a few days later, as soon as everything could be arranged. Of course Mother, as could be expected, was less than enamored with the whole idea.

"I've never heard of anything so ridiculous in my life," she confided in me when we were back home on our own. "This professor, a medical doctor, a respected psychiatrist, is going to experiment with your father and a lot of chimpanzees? I just don't believe it! And why didn't you tell me if you knew about it?"

"I didn't know exactly what he was planning. Oh give it a chance Mum. Professor Meyerhofer knows what he's doing. Let him try it at least." I must say, whatever about my mother's reaction, I was looking forward to what would be my first ever Chimpanzees' Tea Party, and one which would be held in the most unlikely setting of an Austrian mental hospital. I really did believe in the little old professor, and I felt sure that there was sound psychology behind his seemingly bizarre notions, but as he said himself, we would see.

The next two days were a bit of a holiday for me and Papa. Mum as usual sat at the end of the dining table with her computer and sent emails all day long. But I was determined to get out into the sunshine and lovely Alpine fresh air with Papa and enjoy ourselves. Now my father obviously wasn't a great walker or climber, so the mountains weren't an option, and that suited me just fine, but the town has a fantastic swimming pool complex on the edge of the lake. Here you can swim indoors in one of the pools, or outdoors in the lake, or go between the two by means of a number of slides. This had always been our favourite place ever since we started coming here when I was little and I wanted to see if Dad remembered it.

So the very next day we got our stuff together and headed out into the sunshine for the short walk through the town to the swimming pool complex. We always used to arrive there first, at ten o'clock, and would have the slides to ourselves for the first half an hour. Sheer bliss. And so it was this morning, just me and Papa sliding down into the cold water, walking up the steps to the top again in the sun,

232

and sliding back down again, over and over again. I've said it before about people in catatonic trances - they never get tired of repeating the same thing. Normally my Dad would have been the first to have had enough of sliding and want to go dry off and lie in the sun. But not today, today he would have kept going up and down, up and down, all day long.

We had our lunch - chips from the pool bar - sitting in the sun, and then, guess what we did? Yup, up and down the slides again. Since he went into this monkey phase there wasn't an awful lot Dad liked to do, but when he found something he liked, he really did stick to it. I was delighted to see him enjoying himself so much, but it wasn't what I wanted. It was a poor substitute for the real thing; nothing but a complete cure and return to normality would do. While we were there I got a text from Mum saying Prof Meyerhofer wanted the three of us at the hospital at 9.00 the following morning. This is it, I thought, by this time tomorrow we will know. Then I joined Dad on the slides again.

****

Another taxi to the hospital early the following morning, and we just had time to take a deep breath of the still, warm, early morning air, and for me and Mum to give each other a "Here goes" look, before we were into the endless corridors with their innumerable locked doors and found ourselves back in Prof Meyerhofer's office. There he was again in his white coat, with his big head and huge eyes, two years later, and nothing had changed in his life; in ours, so much had changed but not yet enough.

"Ah, Mrs Yones and Miss Yones," (Papa had waited outside with the nurse again) "Thank you so much for coming and for bringing me my favourite and most amazing patient. Yes there is no doubt that Mr Yones has been the most fascinating and most famous patient I have ever treated. The concert pianist, the financial trader, all he has achieved, it is quite remarkable. But all that is over and that is not what we want for him now. Am I right? Now what we want is to get back Mr Yones the ordinary husband and father and teacher and not so successful piano player and trader, am I right? So everything is ready for my experiment and in a few moments we will go through to the back of this building where we have set everything up with some help from my colleagues and of course our animal friends from Vienna. Now please listen very carefully to my instructions. You must at all times do exactly as I say and not interfere with the experiment in any way. We are having a Birthday Party for Mr Yones. We are singing the Happy Birthday song just as his friends did when he was eight or ten years old. Then we are having the Chimp-anzees' Tea Party and we are seeing what is happening. Before we start I am putting Mr Jones into a state of hyp-nosis to help with the suggestions we are making. Come now both of you and not be feeling nervous."

I looked at Mum as we followed the Professor out the door and could see we were both thinking the same thing - not be feeling nervous, he must be joking!

Papa was sitting in another room with a nurse and the Professor went in and stood before him. Then he put his hands on my father's head and said, "You will go into a deep sleep and do everything I say. It is your birthday today and we are having a Birthday Party for you. All your friends are here and they are singing Happy Birthday and you will be having your tea. Now come with us."

Coming out of the room the Professor nodded to us to indicate satisfaction and I took a look at Papa but he seemed the same as usual. We then made our way through a part of the hospital I had never seen before until we were in a large room with a view over the garden. And there in the middle of the garden, seated around a big table, were some of the other hospital staff. We did what we were told and sat down where there were empty chairs and Papa was put at the head of the table. As soon as we were seated a nurse appeared carrying a big cake with lots of lighted candles on a tray and it was placed on the table before my father. I kept my eyes on Papa the whole time and he was utterly entranced. Not only that, but his face wore an expression of complete innocent enjoyment; it might have been the effects of the hypnosis, but he looked just like a child. And then everyone started singing:

Happy Birthday to you
You live in the Zoo
You look like a monkey
And you smell like one too!

And as we all sang, Mum and I joining in as instructed, I could see my father's face cloud over, and a look begin building up, a look of ever-increasing anger. A few shouts of "Happy Birthday Monkey Face" and "He really does look like a monkey" only served to increase the rage in my father's face until I began to be afraid, and so, as I saw looking over at her, was Mum. But we obeyed our instructions and just sat there saying nothing. The nurse who had brought in the cake stayed beside Dad and told him to blow out the candles. He did what he was told and the nurse said, "Good boy Jack, well done, Mummy's very proud of you."

Then all the hospital staff started singing the Happy Birthday song again and calling him Monkey Face a few more times until I thought my father was going to explode. Still he sat there saying nothing, but with his face getting more and more purple. Suddenly, at a signal from the Professor, all the staff got up from the table and as I looked around to see what they were doing, I saw them returning from the building, each one carrying a chimpanzee dressed up in the cutest little clothes of suits and ties or dresses. They deposited the chimps on the chairs which they had vacated and the Professor motioned to us to get up and leave the table. Then the staff started serving the chimps with tea and cakes and buns and drinks and pretty soon they were having a wild time, getting stuck into all this yummy food.

I thought Dad would have liked being surrounded by his simian friends but he still had this ferocious look on his face as if he wanted to burst. Standing around the table the staff kept up the taunting cries of "Happy Birthday Monkey Face," and "You really do smell like a monkey," and every other insult they could think of. Finally my father could take no more. He stood up, slammed both fists down into the cake in front of him, breaking all the candles and sending cream and icing flying everywhere, and for the first time in two years, very slowly, one word at a time, quietly at first, but his voice building up in volume to a ferocious roar, he spoke:

"I -
"Am -
"Not -
"A -
"MONKEY !!!"

Just then I saw something flying across the table and land on Papa. Someone had thrown one of the chimps at him and as he put his arms up in an instinctive reaction of defence, it screeched and Papa yelled and for a moment I couldn't make out what had happened. The chimp they had thrown at Papa landed on the table, right in the middle of what was left of the cake. Then the other chimps ran riot, throwing buns and cake at each other, and emptying drinks over each other's heads. In spite of my initial shock it soon became hilarious and we couldn't help but start laughing. I looked over at Papa and he was holding his arm but laughing too. Not only that, he was pointing at the chimps and talking non-stop, saying things like, "Look at that one he's got a big piece of cake and he's going to throw it at -

yeah there it goes, oh lovely, right in that female chimp's face, watch out mister you're going to get a drink poured over you, oh too late sorry I tried to warn you, Judy did you see that? Oh that's brilliant, yeah sit in it, beautiful, Jenny, how would you like to have to do the laundry for this lot? Oh yeah, nice one, right on his head ... beautiful!"

The staff started picking up the chimps and taking them away for a bath presumably and still Dad wouldn't stop talking. Me and Mum went up to him and gave him the biggest hug and he was still at it, "What, what's with the hugs? What are you both looking at me like that for? Oh I think one of them bit me, my arm seems to be bleeding, here comes a doctor with a big needle, I suppose that's a tetanus shot just like the one I got when I was ten, OK better safe than sorry ... Ow! that hurt more than the chimp bite, here bring back that chimp I want to bite him back, see how he likes it, where are they all gone? That was hilarious, I want to see it again. Who are you? Hi, Jack Jones, nice to meet you, where are we anyway, is this the Zoo, it's really changed around here, where are the other animals? Hi nice to meet you ... " And on and on he went like this incessantly.

Then the Professor joined us and I could see from the big smile on his face that he felt his experiment had been a complete success.

"Don't be concerned about all the talking, that is quite normal I assure you. After a while he will settle down and be himself again. Meanwhile he might be a little talkative but since he hasn't spoken at all in two years, he has a lot of catching up to do."

A *little* talkative! My father had spent two years being Harpo Marx and now he was talking twice as much as Groucho. He hardly stopped to draw breath for the next twenty-four hours, but as predicted he gradually returned to normal. Before we left we tried our best to thank the little old professor but there was nothing we could say which could express how we felt. And any time I tried I just burst into tears. Papa kept saying, "What's Judy crying for?" and "There she goes again, what's with the water-works?" and then he'd say something like, "Who's this nice old man in the white coat. Hi, Jack Jones, pleased to meet you, have we met, you look familiar." And I didn't know whether to laugh or cry so I did both at the same time and that got Papa really confused.

We finally left the hospital and the three of us walked home together, Dad having lost the funny monkey-walk, standing up straight and looking exactly as before. He commented on everything we passed on the way, remembering everything, laughing, joking as usual, just like old times. I for once never opened my mouth, just wanting to listen to my father's voice, his beautiful, funny, familiar voice that I hadn't heard in exactly two years. Heaven!

****

We spent the next three days doing our own bit of rehabilitation with Dad. As predicted by the Professor he remembered nothing of the past two years, and thought he had just woken up after fainting in the apartment. We

239

brought him in to see Professor Meyerhofer one last time so he could make sure there had been a complete cure. Leaving Papa outside the office with the nurse one last time, he explained:

"It is perfectly normal that Mr Yones will not recall anything that has been happening for the last two years. That is not a problem though he may gradually get his memory back. In fact in his case it is better that he does not remember everything all at once as there was so much happening in that time it would be too much for him to comprehend. You can however, try gently reminding him of things if you like, one thing at a time, but if he cannot remember yet it does not matter."

"Believe me Professor," said my mother, "There is a lot of what happened over the past two years that *I* would like to forget."

"How is his arm feeling after the bite of the chimpanzee? I am sorry for doing that, but I was sure the shock and sudden pain were a necessary part of the experiment. That chimp was specially trained to give a little bite."

"His arm seems fine," Mum replied, "It certainly was worth it to get him to come out of the trance."

"If I'd known that was all it would take I would have bitten him myself," I added.

Back outside in the sunshine we said goodbye for the very last time and walked home again. I was really sad leaving the funny old professor, and gave him a big hug.

"We can never thank you enough for what you have done for us," I said. "I will never forget you."

"My dear child," said the professor. "It is I who should be thanking you. This has been such a wonderful experience for me meeting you and your family. Your father's was the most interesting case of my whole career, and you have shown such bravery and loyalty in one so young it is just remarkable. Good-bye my dear Mrs Yones and Miss Yones, I wish you all happiness and successes in the future. And please to keep in touch with any newses about my favourite patient."

"Don't worry," said my mother, "You won't be hearing anything as we plan on having a very quiet life from now on."

The following day we got into a taxi outside our apartment and left for Salzburg. Dad and I were in the back as usual and in order to prove to myself that everything was real, I tried my own little experiment, and sat there staring at him. The result was perfect and exactly as predicted:

"Hey whatcha starin at?" he said, "You creepin me out!"

"I had a funny feeling you were going to say that," I replied, smiling.

Then we started playing a game where I tried to remind him of some of the things that had happened over the past two years.

"Do you remember meeting the Prime Minister and the Chancellor of the Exchequer at No 11 Downing Street?"

"No."

"Do you remember playing the piano in Carnegie Hall and starting a riot that got into all the newspapers?"

"No."

"Do you remember climbing down the scaffolding on the outside of the Houses of Parliament?"

"That's enough Judy, stop it now, don't pay any attention to her Jack, she's only joking."

"I know that," he replied, "If I had done any of those things I think I might have remembered."

A couple of hours later we were on the plane, sitting at the back again, soon after take-off.

"I think I'll have the full breakfast," said Papa. "It feels like it's been a while since I had that."

"Thought you might," I said.

"Some things never change," said Mum.

"And I hope they never will," I added. I looked at my two wonderful parents beside me and I was so happy that everything was back to normal again and we were going home.

****

We never did find out exactly what caused the initial brainstorm or fit or whatever you want to call it that sent Papa into his trance, and I suppose we never will know. My own feeling is that after so many years of failure and frustration and rage at himself and the world he just snapped. His conscious mind couldn't take any more; he had had too much reality when the reality was so painful. You see he always had the ability to play the piano and to be a successful trader, it was just all his fears and emotional baggage and the thirty years of perceived failure that were the problem. Maybe his subconscious mind knew that it could succeed where his conscious mind had held him back, and it desperately wanted and needed to succeed. Maybe his subconscious wanted out.

I suppose in the end the fact is that he was happy being the Monkey Man, happy and successful for the first time in his life. For the first time in his life he succeeded at the only two things he ever wanted to achieve. It's just a pity he wasn't around in any real sense to appreciate it. But at the same time, the appalling illness that took away his mind and stripped him of his human dignity, also, in one of the ironies life is famed for, gave him everything he wanted. That's why I have agreed to the title of the book and I will let the publishers have their way. Anyway he did love monkeys; we both did, they were always our favourite animal, from going to the zoo when I was really small to the games we would play together every night in my bedroom. And even if a monkey wasn't responsible for taking him away from us, it was definitely a monkey - or rather a chimp - that brought him back. So this is for you, Papa, father, Monkey Man, to tell you how much I love you, and to thank you for everything you've given me.

Loveyouforever
Your little Judy

The End

Printed in Great Britain
by Amazon

85005246R00140